Shade's Lady

Also from Joanna Wylde

Reaper's Property
Reaper's Legacy
Devil's Game
Silver Bastard
Reaper's Fall
Reaper's Fire
Reapers and Bastards

Coming June 2017:
Taz (Book 1 of the Devil's Jacks MC series)

Shade's Lady

A Reapers MC Novella

By Joanna Wylde

1001 Dark Nights

Shade's Lady
A Reapers MC Novella
By Joanna Wylde

1001 Dark Nights

ISBN: 978-1-945920-33-2

Published by Evil Eye Concepts, Incorporated

Acknowledgments from the Author

Thank you so much to Rebecca Zanetti, who connected me to 1001 Dark Nights. It's a wonderful thing when you meet someone who's smart, funny and not afraid to share a celebratory drink at noon. Long live the booth!

Thanks also to Cara Carnes, Kylie Scott and Jen Frederick for their critiques, as well as Margarita, Jess and Lori for being foolish enough to volunteer (again) when I needed help (again). Ladies, you kick ass and I appreciate everything you've done so much. (Except for you, Kylie. You are The Worst.)

Finally, thanks to Liz Berry, Kimberly Guidroz, Kasi Alexander, Fedora Chen, Pam Jamison and the entire 1001 Dark Nights family. Working on this book with you has been a joy and a pleasure.

Sign up for the 1001 Dark Nights Newsletter
and be entered to win a Tiffany Key necklace.

There's a contest every month!

Go to www.1001DarkNights.com to subscribe.

As a bonus, all subscribers will receive a free
1001 Dark Nights story
The First Night
by Lexi Blake & M.J. Rose

One Thousand and One Dark Nights

Once upon a time, in the future…

I was a student fascinated with stories and learning. I studied philosophy, poetry, history, the occult, and the art and science of love and magic. I had a vast library at my father's home and collected thousands of volumes of fantastic tales.

I learned all about ancient races and bygone times. About myths and legends and dreams of all people through the millennium. And the more I read the stronger my imagination grew until I discovered that I was able to travel into the stories... to actually become part of them.

I wish I could say that I listened to my teacher and respected my gift, as I ought to have. If I had, I would not be telling you this tale now.
But I was foolhardy and confused, showing off with bravery.

One afternoon, curious about the myth of the Arabian Nights, I traveled back to ancient Persia to see for myself if it was true that every day Shahryar (Persian: شهريار*, "king") married a new virgin, and then sent yesterday's wife to be beheaded. It was written and I had read, that by the time he met Scheherazade, the vizier's daughter, he'd killed one thousand women.*

Something went wrong with my efforts. I arrived in the midst of the story and somehow exchanged places with Scheherazade – a phenomena that had never occurred before and that still to this day, I cannot explain.

Now I am trapped in that ancient past. I have taken on Scheherazade's life and the only way I can protect myself and stay alive is to do what she did to protect herself and stay alive.

Every night the King calls for me and listens as I spin tales. And when the evening ends and dawn breaks, I stop at a point that leaves him breathless and yearning for more. And so the King spares my life for one more day, so that he might hear the rest of my dark tale.

As soon as I finish a story... I begin a new one... like the one that you, dear reader, have before you now.

Chapter One

Violetta, Idaho
Tuesday afternoon

Mandy

"Did you get my text?" Sara asked, pushing through the office door. I'd just finished tying my apron around my waist, and was leaning toward the cracked mirror on the wall for one last makeup check before punching in.

"No," I replied, frowning. "Dropped my cell in the toilet this morning. I called the phone people. They said I didn't have any insurance, so I'm fucked. I put it on Future Me's list of things to worry about."

Sadly, Future Me's list got longer every day. She was supposed to pay our credit card bill, figure out whether we should break up with our boyfriend, and find a better place to sleep than my sister's couch. She also needed to lose ten pounds and magically fix the rusted-out Kia Sedona currently broken down in my sister's yard. Present Me would've felt guilty about dumping all this on the poor thing, but I only had three minutes left to punch in and start slinging drinks for drunken bikers, so it would just have to wait.

Yup. I'm organized like that.

Studying my reflection, I ran an eye down the length of my body. Tight tank with a hint of bra showing? Check. (Nothing like some boob action to bring in the tips. Not only that, Rebel had said he'd be here tonight, and he always liked seeing the girls.) Lipstick was bright and shiny, no smudges on the teeth. More eye makeup than I'd usually wear, but ever since I'd started hanging out with Rebel's biker friends, I'd kicked it up a notch. Made me look wild and sexy. Not gonna lie—I liked this new me. I liked her a lot. I guess if there was one good thing about my sister's life falling apart—and me moving to Violetta to help with the kids—it was that it'd forced me to change my life, too.

"Shitty about the phone," Sara said. "No pun intended. I got stuck washing glasses this afternoon. Now my hands are all chapped. We were so busy that I didn't get to take my break, so I couldn't run out to pick up some lotion. Was hoping you could bring some in with you."

"Sorry."

My fellow waitress ran a hand through her blonde hair, then gave it a shake. Her impressive rack shook at the same time, and I sighed, feeling a little jealous. Sara's girls were big and bountiful. No push-up on earth could ever make my modest rack compete. Still, my jeans were tight, my bra was red, and I'd recently run fresh out of fucks to give.

Life could be worse.

"I wish I had your tits," I told Sara.

She laughed. "I wish I had your butt. Just think of it—we could form one perfect waitress and turn into an unstoppable tip-earning machine."

I giggled. "So where do I fall on the slut scale?"

Sara studied me thoughtfully.

"I think right around a seven," she said, nodding in approval. "Slutty enough to make bank on tips, but not full-on club whore. If it's your goal to make Rebel horny as hell by the end of your shift, you're right on target. We gotta get out there, though. It's gonna be a crazy busy night. We'll work our asses off but at least we won't be bored."

"Works for me," I said, giving her a wink in the mirror. "If there's one thing I hate, it's being bored. Although Rebel better watch himself. I caught him groping some other girl last night while he thought I was in the stock room. He keeps that shit up, I don't care how horny he gets—he's on his own."

Sara raised a brow. "You think he's cheating?"

I turned to her, shrugging unhappily.

"I don't have anything solid," I admitted. "But something feels off to me. I mean, he's a huge flirt—we all know that."

"Most of them are."

"Yeah," I agreed. "So it's hard to know how much of it's just him being him or if there's more going on. He's been acting weird, though. I don't know… I guess I'll figure it out sooner or later. You know what's really lame?"

"What's that?"

"I feel like a total bitch saying this, but in some ways I think I'd miss riding with his club more than I'd miss Rebel. If we broke up, I mean."

Sara snorted.

"There's a whole bar full of bikers out there," she pointed out. "And don't think they haven't noticed that cute butt of yours. Rebel's a fun guy, but if he turns out to be a dick, it's not like he's your only option. Hell, you could just buy your own motorcycle. There's no law saying only men can ride—Rebel's club is just a bunch of weekend warriors. Real clubs like the Reapers may be all hardass about women as members, but there are riding clubs for girls, too. Those Ladies of Harley seem to be having a pretty good time. They certainly party enough to keep up with the boys."

I giggled. "I can't even afford a new cell phone, let alone a motorcycle."

Sara winked at me, then her eyes caught the clock and they widened.

"Oh, *fuck!* Look at the time. You got about two seconds to punch in or Bone will shit bricks."

Diving for the time clock, I grabbed my card and shoved it into the machine, then held it up triumphantly.

"Made it!"

"Great. Now get out there and sell some drinks," she said. "And remember—don't be afraid to show off that red bra. I need you to buy a new phone. This lack of communication is seriously fucking with my night. Now I have lizard fingers and no lotion."

She raised her hands like claws and gave a mock roar. Laughing, I pushed out the door and started down the hallway, because Sara was definitely right about one thing—I really did need a new phone, and I'd be damned if I'd ask my sister for a loan to buy one. I'd moved to Bumfuck Nowhere to help her and the kids, not to mooch. I was big on personal responsibility these days, unlike my ex-husband (who was hopefully burning in hell).

That's what you get for marrying someone named Trevor.

The bar was hopping by the time I made it to the floor and Bone—bartender, owner and all around scary guy—shoved a tray of drinks at me before I even had time to look over the table assignments.

"We've got the Reapers coming in," he said, his voice blunt and harsh. "They'll be in the back room. That means we'll have a different kind of crowd tonight. Less mom and pop bikers and more wannabes and hangarounds. Could be interesting. Don't fuck up."

"You always make me feel so special and wanted," I said, wrinkling my nose at him. Bone grunted, but I saw a hint of humor in his eyes. He was a good guy, despite the whole prize-fighter vibe he had going for him. The Pit was a biker bar, which meant flirting came with the job, yet he always took care of his girls. All we had to do was say the word and he'd throw out anyone who got too handsy.

Grabbing the tray, I carried it across the room, ducking and weaving around big guys wearing leather and sexy babes in tight shirts. Everyone was laughing and having fun, which was one of my favorite things about working here. These guys came to the Pit for a good time, and that's exactly what we gave them—booze, music, a little bit of dancing and a whole lot of action.

Throw in the fact that my sister's place was only a couple miles away and the job was a perfect fit.

The first hour of my shift passed in a blur, busy enough that I didn't notice the time but not so busy people got pissy waiting for their drinks. I'd just leaned across the bar to give Bone a fresh order when the door opened and the room quieted.

The Reapers Motorcycle Club had arrived.

There were probably ten of them total, dressed in leather and patches and so much pure badassery it radiated through the room like a shock wave. I halfway expected heavy metal theme music to start playing spontaneously. I'd met a few of them before—they had a chapter over in Cranston, which was only thirty miles from Violetta. Rebel's riding club had hosted a barbecue last month, and the Reapers had come with all their assorted old ladies and hangers-on.

At the time, I'd been startled at how everyone treated them—almost like visiting royalty. Now I knew a lot more about biker culture, including the fact that in the world of casual riding clubs, true outlaws like the Reapers really *were* royalty.

Then their king walked in, and everyone got real quiet.

Shade.

He surveyed the bar, radiating a kind of cold, icy authority that gave me the shivers every time I saw him. When I first met Rebel, I'd teased him about having a crush on Shade because my new boyfriend couldn't stop talking about the man. Then I'd met Shade in person. Now I got it. Rebel worked hard to make sure everyone knew he was a big, bad biker.

Shade didn't have to work at it.

He just *was* big and bad.

According to Bone, Shade was the youngest national president in Reapers Motorcycle Club history. One of the girls at the barbecue told me he was a killer. Apparently he'd been arrested for murder, then gotten off on a technicality. Not that this seemed to bother her. She'd been all breathless and sighing, and later I'd spotted Shade pushing her up against a tree, skirt around her waist. He'd been devouring her mouth while she frantically clawed at his pants.

Apparently the whole murderer thing wasn't a deal breaker.

Shade's eyes caught mine, and I froze, feeling like he could see all the way down to my soul. In that instant, I completely understood why that girl had let him fuck her against a tree. The man radiated power, strength and raw sex. He was the biggest, nastiest bastard in the room—not to mention easy on the eyes—and deep down inside I just knew we'd make beautiful babies together. Too bad I already sort of had a boyfriend… Shade was so potent we'd probably have quintuplets or something crazy on the first try.

You don't even want *a baby,* I reminded my quivering ovaries.

Jump him! Jump him and ride him like a cowgirl! they snapped back. *Just think how sexy and strong he is. His sperm could kick Rebel's ass and you know it!*

"Go tell them the back room's ready," Bone said, breaking my trance. "Make sure they're settled. By the time you're out, I'll have their drinks ready to go."

"Me?" I asked, stomach clenching. Shade might be pretty to look at, but he scared the shit out of me—I'd decided about five minutes after meeting him and his club brothers that I'd best keep my distance.

Shade caught my fear from across the room, and his lip quirked. Not quite a smile. More like the amused, tolerant smirk a cat gives a doomed mouse. Made me want to run and hide in a corner.

But I had the feeling that no one ever successfully hid from Shade.

"Yeah," Bone said. "You've got the experience and Sara hasn't had a break all night. Suz just punched in but I don't trust her in there with them—she's looking for an old man, and her lips flap too much. Just serve the drinks, do what you're told and if you happen to overhear anything, you keep your fucking mouth shut. Got me?"

I broke away from Shade's gaze and turned to my boss. His face was serious. Dead serious. I swallowed.

"Are they—"

"Stop," he said, cutting me off. "Whatever you're thinking, just stop. Thinking isn't part of your job here. Neither is flirting. Not tonight. You carry drinks, you take away empties, you hear nothing and you say nothing. Easy money, babe. Go earn it."

He handed me a set of keys and gave me a small shove. I started across the room toward the bikers, ready to escort them despite the fact that they obviously knew exactly where they were going.

"Hi," I said, smiling uncertainly. "I'm—"

"Mandy," Shade said, eyes sweeping down my figure. I got the sense that he saw everything in that glance, from the red bra just peeking out of the top of my tank top to the fact that my ex-husband had gotten me arrested last year. "I know who you are. We met at the barbecue, remember?"

Oh, I remembered all right. He'd caught me by a belt loop on my jeans, pulling me just close enough for our bodies to brush against each other. Then he'd whispered I'd be welcome on the back of his bike any time.

Somehow, I'd managed to squeak out that I had a boyfriend.

Shade had laughed, running one finger under my chin, tilting my head up toward his. "That's your problem, baby. You don't need a boy—you need a man. Call me when you're ready."

Just the memory was enough to turn my face neon red. Thankfully, Bone was the kind of boss who believed a dimly-lit bar is a good bar, so hopefully it wasn't too obvious to the badass standing in front of me.

"Great to see you again," I told him, and I'm proud to say my voice didn't squeak this time. "I'll be your waitress tonight. Bone is pouring drinks right now."

"Thanks, babe," Shade said. "Lead the way."

I started toward the back of the room, feeling the weight of his eyes the entire time. Well, either that or I was hallucinating, which was also a realistic possibility. The man was too potent for his own good—like catnip for women. Too many pheromones or some such. It really wasn't my fault that he'd drugged me with his sexiness. Fortunately, I was smart and knew better.

(Fingers crossed.)

We reached the back room, and I fumbled with the keys to unlock the door. It wasn't part of the bar proper, although there were tables and chairs back here. Bone used it for large groups and occasionally storage. For some reason I couldn't get the key into the little hole, and the fact that Shade stood right behind me—radiating heat and pure fuckability, the bastard—wasn't helping. Then his hand reached around mine, grasping the key and sliding it into the door with a slow, sure motion.

You know, that's probably how he'd—

Shut up! I screeched mentally at my idiotic girl parts. *You have a boyfriend and this guy is a murderer. Or something. Definitely* something. *NO quintuplets for you.*

The door swung open. Apparently Bone had known they were coming, because the smaller tables had been shoved together to make one long surface, and the boxes that'd been in here yesterday were gone.

Shade caught my hips in his hands, gently pushing me to the side as his biker brothers filed in past him. I waited for him to let go but he didn't. He decided to run his thumbs up and under the side of my tank instead. I shivered.

"I'll be right back with your drinks," I said, hoping Bone knew what they wanted because my brain had stopped working. The last thing I needed was a bunch of Reapers pissed off at me for fucking up their order. Shade didn't drop his hands, just loosened his grip and lowered his head, taking in my scent.

My nipples went tight and he gave a low chuckle. Then he dropped his hands, brushing past me without a second glance.

"Sounds good, babe," he said, stepping into the room. "Shut the door behind you."

The evening got weird after that.

The Reapers stationed a guy with a "prospect" patch on his vest outside the door, and every time I came back with more booze he would knock on the door, check, and then let me in like a scene out of *The Godfather*. It would've been funny as hell if they hadn't gotten so quiet every time I walked in. You know, the kind of quiet you get when you're talking about where to bury bodies. Not that I had any reason to think they had bodies to bury, but...well, there was that whole rumor thing.

Oh, and Shade watched me every second, every time I was in there. Like, *watched* me. Enough to creep me out. I'd gone to Bone and asked him if I could swap out with Sara now that she was off break.

"Suck it up," he'd said, crossing his big arms over his chest. "This is your job. Do it. If you're a good girl, you'll get a real nice tip at the end of the night."

"What if I'm not a good girl?" I'd asked, unnerved. "I've never actually been very good at being…well, you know. Good."

Bone grinned at me.

"Then you'll get an even bigger tip."

Somehow that didn't make me feel much better.

"Now go back in there and make sure nobody runs dry. If the Reapers are happy, we're all happy. That's the way this thing works. Unless you want to find a new job?"

I shook my head quickly, unnerved.

"No, I need the work," I assured him.

"What a coincidence, because I need a waitress who follows orders."

"Stop scaring her," Sara said, butting in. Bone glared at her and she glared right back, cocking her hip belligerently.

"Fucking women," he muttered, turning away. Sara laughed, flipping him off behind his back.

"There's a mirror behind the bar, remember? I saw that," he muttered. "You're both fired."

"You love us and you know it."

Bone growled something, then reached for a beer glass, deliberately ignoring us.

"He's right about one thing—you need to get in there and make sure those boys don't run dry," Sara said, lowering her voice. "We can't afford to piss off the Reapers."

"Yeah, I get it."

"Then start moving," she replied, snapping me with the bar towel. It caught me off guard and I laughed, because no matter how scary Shade and his buddies might be, I really liked my job. It certainly wasn't boring, and that was good, right?

Trevor wasn't boring either, and look how that turned out. Remember how bad jail food tastes?

Ah, shit. I did remember. It tasted bad. Real bad. I'd just have to stay focused and not let myself get sucked into anything dangerous. Shouldn't be that hard—it wasn't like serving drinks was all that complicated. All I needed to do was pay attention and keep my nose clean.

Easy as pie.

Chapter Two

Rebel showed up around eleven, looking a little rough around the edges. He'd gone on an epic drinking binge with his buddies the night before, and while I wasn't sure how late they'd been out, he hadn't made it to bed yet when I'd texted him good morning. He was still cute, though, and when he walked in the door and grinned at me with those bright eyes of his, I felt that same happy tingle that'd attracted me to him in the first place. Not quite the same dance my girl parts did when they saw Shade, but it was still good.

Mostly.

Okay, so Rebel was a jerk and a dumbass—oh, and there was the whole potential cheating thing—but somehow he always managed to charm me out of my pants anyway. And it wasn't like I was looking for someone serious anyway. No more real relationships for me.

Not after the Trevor debacle.

"Hey, baby," he said, hooking his good arm around my waist, pulling me in for a kiss. Bone leaned forward on the bar, glaring at me pointedly.

Bone didn't like Rebel.

This was funny because it'd been Rebel who'd helped me get the job here in the first place. Or at least, he'd been the first one to bring me in. I got the job on my own. We'd all been hanging around one afternoon when a group of nearly forty riders showed up out of nowhere. I'd seen the panicked look on Sara's face—it was just her and Bone in the place—and felt terrible. I'd waited enough tables in my life to know she was fucked without more help.

Then I'd gone to the bathroom and found pee all over the floor.

Bone was slammed at the bar, Sara was running her ass off just trying to get everyone water, and I didn't feel like wading through piss to get to the toilet, so I'd found a mop in the back and gone for it. Then I'd taken out the garbage (because it was disgusting) and things kept going from there.

Half an hour later, Bone noticed and offered me a job.

Now I worked here about thirty hours a week, which was almost enough to pay the bills, but not quite. On the other hand, the Pit had the distinct advantage of being fun while not being my old job at the gas station. The gas station where my sister's ex, Handsy Randy the drug dealer, was the manager.

(Don't even get me started on *that* one.)

The bar might be rough and tough, but I felt safer here because I didn't have to worry about Randy's wandering fingers. Oh, and Bone wasn't a passive-aggressive cheating fuckwad who'd abandoned his family.

That was a big plus, too.

"How's your night?" I asked Rebel. He leaned down and gave me another quick kiss. I pulled away from him because I'd already pissed Bone off once.

"Good," Rebel said. "But I'm horny as hell. When's your next break?"

"Why, you think I'm gonna blow you in the parking lot or something?"

"I'd settle for a hand job," he replied, grinning.

"Mandy!" Bone shouted. "You got customers waiting in the back. Move your ass."

"Boss man is calling," I said, giving Rebel a wink. Rebel frowned.

"Who's in the back room?"

"Reapers."

"Really?" he asked, perking up. "Is Shade with them? He's got a bike for sale that I'm interested in. I've given up on mine."

"Oh, it would be great if you got something new," I said, trying not to sound too excited. Rebel's bike had been out of commission for nearly two weeks now, which meant no riding for me. We still hung out with his biker friends, but showing up in a battered pickup truck to a motorcycle rally felt sort of weird.

"Yeah, it looks really good," he said. "You think I can go back there, maybe talk to him?"

"Don't pay you to play with your boyfriend, Mandy!" Bone yelled, and I pulled away from Rebel.

"No idea, I just carry the drinks," I told him. "I gotta run."

Back at the bar, Bone shoved three more pitchers of beer at me, scowling across the pass-through as I grabbed a tray to carry them.

"You can do better than him," he said, jerking his head toward Rebel.

"We're just having fun," I told him. "Got distracted, though."

"Keep your focus," Bone said, then his face softened. "The Reapers are important customers, babe. They own this state. You piss them off and I really will have to fire you, no matter how much we like having you around."

I turned away, then remembered Rebel's question.

"Hey, Bone," I said, catching his attention again. "Not to push, but Rebel's interested in a bike that Shade's selling. Do you think it's okay if he goes back there and tries to talk to him?"

"Don't get involved," Bone replied, his tone final. "Bring them drinks. Take away empties. That's it. Trust me on this."

I raised a brow because that sounded ominous, especially since Shade was trying to sell something. Wouldn't he *want* to talk to a potential buyer? Then again, what the hell did I know? I'd been dating Rebel all of two months. Before that I'd never been on a bike in my life, let along hung out around a real motorcycle club like the Reapers.

"Okey-dokey," I said, carefully balancing the sloshing pitchers as I headed down the hallway. The prospect knocked on the door when

I arrived, poking his head in and then nodding for me to go through. The men were more relaxed now, lounging around the table while they laughed and talked. There weren't any women with them tonight. This was unusual. I set one pitcher on each end of the table, then started snagging empty shot glasses. Shade's eyes followed me, dark and hungry.

I tried to ignore him but it was hard.

His sandy hair was pulled back in a ponytail streaked blond in places from the sun. His arms were tan, and while I spotted the hint of a tattoo peeking out from under one arm of his ragged T-shirt, he wasn't as marked up as most of the bikers who came in. His face was craggy, with just the faintest of lines at the corners of his eyes. They looked good on him. Shooting him a sideways glance, I tried to guess his age.

Early thirties, maybe?

A few years older than me, but still well within my range.

You're not interested in him, moron, so stop thinking like that.

Avoiding his end of the table, I filled my tray and started toward the door.

"You missed one," Shade said, his voice a low rumble. I looked over to find an empty tumbler sitting in front of him, remnants of a whiskey on the rocks I'd served earlier. To grab it, I'd have to either lean across the table and show off my boobs or squeeze in next to him. Neither option was comforting.

Not that he'd cop a feel.

Nope, not Shade.

He was above those kinds of games. But just being in the same room made me feel all weird and unsettled. It was one thing to joke with one of our usual customers or brush a hand across his shoulder. That was just casual flirtation—it didn't mean anything. Shade made promises with his eyes, though. Promises I was afraid he'd keep.

You'd be welcome on the back of my bike any time, babe.

"Tray is full," I told him, offering a tight smile. "Give me five and I'll be back to take care of it."

Turning away, I decided that I needed some air. Wasn't it time for my break? Yeah. I'd tell Bone I needed a break, maybe go make out with Rebel in the parking lot for a few minutes. That'd set me right. Not that he'd be getting his hand job, because I had standards.

Low standards, but they still existed.

I stepped back out into the hallway to find Rebel standing next to the prospect, looking all eager.

"I'll check and see if he has time," the prospect told him, passing me as he ducked into the room.

"Is he in a good mood?" Rebel asked me hopefully.

"Who?"

"Shade," he replied. "Who else?"

Jesus. He really did have a man crush on the guy.

"How would I know?" I said, annoyed. "Hey, I'm gonna go talk to Bone, see if I can take my break now."

"Wait for a minute," Rebel said. "Until after I finish talking to Shade. I've missed you."

He glanced down at my chest pointedly, and I flushed. He had this thing for fucking my boobs, squishing them together around his dick. It wasn't as much fun for me as some of the other games we played, but I loved watching him come. I also loved it when—*nope, don't go there.*

Still, thinking about crawling into bed with my sexy (if annoying) boyfriend was enough to improve my mood. Orgasms will do that for a girl. Balancing the tray against my side with one hand, I ran the other down his chest, glancing down the hallway to make sure we were really alone before giving his dick a quick squeeze. He groaned and I felt tinglies run down my spine. The door opened and we jumped apart.

"Shade says he'll talk to you," the prospect told him. Then he turned to me. "He also says they're good on drinks, at least for now. You can check back in about half an hour."

Rebel pushed past me so fast I nearly dropped the tray of empties. So much for his boob fetish. The tinglies evaporated and I sighed, heading back down the hall. Rebel might be fun to hang out with, but the guy was never gonna be my soul mate. *You don't have to marry the man to enjoy each other,* I reminded myself, mentally adding "find soul mate" to Future Me's list.

Then I mentally crossed it off, because fuck soul mates.

My sister and I had both struck out once already, and that was enough. Future Me would probably do better to stay single. I should add *that* to her list.

Bone put me to work washing glasses. The bar crowd had thinned out and Sara had already gone home for the night. Suz was doing surprisingly well handling the customers on her own. I'd just finished draining the sink when I saw that the garbage was getting full. I decided to be proactive and go dump it. Lifting it out of the can, I ducked through the side door and jogged down the steps and across the gravel toward the dumpster. I caught a flash of motion from the corner of my eye and looked over to see three men standing next to the building.

One leaned casually against the wall toward the back of the bar. Next to him was a second, his stance vigilant, while a third stood in front of them, waving his hands and talking. Then I caught a familiar voice in the breeze.

Rebel?

Holy shit, that was Rebel out there. Was he talking to Shade? I squinted my eyes, thinking I really needed to get myself some new contacts. Yup, that was Shade, and another one of his biker buddies whose name I couldn't quite remember. I made a point of letting the dumpster lid slam down hard after tossing in the garbage. That way they'd know I hadn't been trying to spy on them. Then I went back to washing dishes, hoping Rebel wasn't getting himself in trouble.

He came back inside about ten minutes later, looking distracted but pleased. I caught his gaze and raised a brow, silently asking him how things had gone. Rebel grinned and gave me a thumbs-up. I wasn't quite sure what that meant in practical terms, but at least he was happy.

"Can you grab Bone? Shade needs to talk to him."

I looked up, startled to find the prospect standing in the open walkway at the end of the bar.

"Um, sure," I said. "Give me a sec."

Bone was at the far end of the bar, flirting with a very drunk, very friendly girl whose tank top was so tight it might as well have been painted on. I caught my boss's arm. He turned to me, frowning.

"Sorry, but Shade wants to see you in the back."

"Won't be long," he told Drunk Girl. She pouted as he started down the hall, then narrowed her eyes at me.

"Are you with him or something?"

"With who?" I asked, confused.

"Bone."

I burst out laughing, then shook my head.

"Nope, I don't think I'm his type."

She looked me over, and I couldn't help but notice that she didn't look so drunk now. Interesting. Someone was playing games, trying to catch Bone's attention. "And what's his type?"

"Drunk and pretty," I said, offering her a smile. "Keep up the good work and he'll be all yours."

That seemed to make her happy, which felt nice. It'd be interesting to see if Bone went home with her. He lived in an apartment right over the bar, but I'd never seen him take a woman there. I'd asked him about it once and he said it was too hard to get rid of them when he was done.

Yeah, my boss was classy like that.

One of the regulars shouted for beer, and I'd just finished pulling his pint when Bone showed up again, looking pissed. He stomped over to me, glaring.

"You're done for the night," he said. I stared at him, confused.

"What do you mean?"

"Grab your shit and punch out," he replied. "Your shift is over."

This made no sense.

"You're going to close by yourself?"

"Suz is here," he snapped.

"But Suz has never closed before."

And I need the hours…

"Not your problem. Leave. Now. And watch your ass, okay?"

The warning confused me even more.

"What's going on?"

"Not a Goddamned thing," he muttered. "Just me running my bar all by my fucking lonesome. Christ."

He ran a hand through his hair, obviously frustrated as he glanced toward Drunk Girl, then sighed. Okey-dokey. Whatever was happening here, it was way over my pay grade. I turned to leave, then thought about my poor drowned cell phone. Turning back, I asked, "Can you give me an extra shift this week? I mean, since you're sending me home early?"

"We'll see," he replied, looking even more frustrated. "Depends."

"On what?"

"On how many more fucking questions you ask."

Well, that was confusing and bizarre all mashed together. Great. Trying not to scowl, I headed for the office, untying my apron as I walked. The prospect was gone and the back room had been abandoned. Had the Reapers gone out the back door? I stepped in, looking at the table. It was covered with empty glasses but no money to pay for their booze. Not even a tip.

Fuck.

I knew Bone sent them drinks on the house sometimes, but they'd always left something for me. Now I'd lost my hours *and* gotten stiffed.

"Fucking men."

Five minutes later I'd punched out, grabbing my bag as I went to look for Rebel. He met me coming down the hallway, obviously excited. I opened my mouth to ask about his talk with Shade. Before I could say anything, he caught me up into his arms, giving me a hard, smacking kiss.

"Gonna get the bike," he said when it ended, eyes still dancing. "But I need your help picking it up. Shade wants to take care of things tonight. That's why he asked Bone to let you off work."

Ah, crapsicles. That explained Bone's general pissiness about sending me home.

"You should've talked to me first," I said, frowning. "I can't afford to—"

"It's all good," Rebel insisted. "Bone won't hold it against you, I promise. But I really need your help. I've got my truck here. We're gonna head to Shade's place and pick up the bike, and then I need you to drive the truck back home for me."

"Can't we go in the morning?" I asked, annoyed. "It seems weird that we have to do this in the middle of the night."

Rebel flushed.

"He gave me a discount, okay?" he admitted. "Way better deal than I expected. I'm scared he'll change his mind. We get it done tonight, it's done. You'll love the new bike, I promise. We're gonna have a blast on it."

"Okay," I said. "But you owe me."

"Anything you want, baby. I promise. Just do this one favor for me. I swear you won't regret it."

Grabbing my hand, he dragged me down the hall, through the bar and into the parking lot. Lined up across the front were the Reapers MC bikes, flanked by Shade and his brothers. Most of them were busy getting ready to leave, but Shade stood staring at us, his big arms crossed over his chest in the dim glow of the single streetlight.

"Oh, I forgot one thing," Rebel said, pausing on the porch. He turned me toward him, frowning apologetically. "I've got a bunch of shit in the front seat of the truck. Boxes and stuff that can't go in the back, so there's no room for you. I need you to catch a ride with Shade, sound good?"

My eyes widened, and I stiffened.

"No, that's not *good,*" I hissed in a low voice, glancing toward the man in question, hoping he couldn't read lips. Offending him wasn't the brightest, but neither was climbing on his bike.

Way too scary.

Rebel caught my shoulders, giving me a little squeeze as he stared deep into my eyes. "I'm sorry, babe. I really am. But I need your help tonight, so please say you'll do it? Just this once? It's not even that far."

I looked back toward Shade, who watched us, his face expressionless. The man was terrifying, no question, but would it really kill me to take a quick ride with him?

"You'll be right behind us the whole time?" I asked Rebel, frustrated. But it wasn't actually that big of a deal, was it? I'd already clocked out for the night and since I'd planned on pulling a full shift, it wasn't like I'd had anything else going on. Rebel nodded.

"Right behind you," he said. "No worries. But you better get your ass over there. He's waiting, and he's not the most patient of guys."

With that, Rebel turned me toward the steps and pushed me forward, giving me a little slap on the butt. Usually I thought that was fun and cute, but it wasn't nearly so fun and cute with the Reapers as our audience. Taking a deep breath, I steeled myself to face Shade.

It's no big deal, Mandy. Just one quick ride. Get over yourself.

Chapter Three

"You okay with this?" Shade asked, looming over me. He didn't look like a man who was happy because he'd just sold a bike. He was clearly in a shit mood, and that frown of his would've sent children screaming.

Hell, it nearly sent *me* screaming.

Suck it up, Mandy. No big deal. You've dealt with guys worse than him before.

Hmm… Wasn't entirely sure that was accurate. My ex—Trevor—had been a jackass and a petty criminal, but if those murder rumors were true, he was nothing compared to Shade. Of course, Shade hadn't gotten me thrown in jail and sentenced to probation, so that was a point in his favor.

I swallowed, glancing at his intimidatingly large maroon Harley. The Harley I'd soon be riding. I wondered how it would feel to cradle his ass in my hips and immediately got tinglies. Yup, those were definitely tinglies. I just couldn't quite decide if they were tinglies of fear or—

It's only a ride, I reminded myself. *Probably won't even take very long. Then we can go home and I can have a little talk with Rebel about boundaries, and how he shit all over mine.*

"Yeah, sure. It's no big deal," I said, trying to keep the words light. The fact that my voice cracked halfway through probably didn't help my case.

Shade cocked his head, staring me down.

"You sure?"

I glanced toward Rebel, who nodded eagerly. Right now he wasn't looking very cute, I decided. Not very cute at all.

"I said it's fine," I told Shade, and this time my voice held steady.

"We leaving, boss?" one of the other Reapers asked. Another big guy. Did they make these bikers in any other size? His vest patches declared his name was Dopey and that he was something called a road captain. I looked him up and down, deciding that he looked less like one of the seven dwarfs than anyone I'd ever seen in my entire life—and I'd spotted Dolph Lundgren in the Las Vegas airport once.

"Guess so," Shade said. "You're with me, little waitress."

I sort of wanted to protest this, but mostly I wanted the whole thing over, so I climbed up behind him on the motorcycle. He kicked it to life with a roar, the bikes slowly pulling out in formation with ours in the front rank. Rebel shot me another thumbs-up as we passed.

I'd have flipped him off, but Shade gave the throttle a twist and the powerful machine leapt forward with a burst of speed that had me holding his waist tight with both hands. Then we were tearing down the highway, the sound of engines splitting the night.

Rebel had insisted that we wouldn't be going far. As the miles passed, I started to realize that his definition of "far" and mine might be slightly different. Given that I'd only lived in the area for about six months, it wasn't like I recognized any landmarks at night.

I didn't know how long we'd been riding when I started to look at mile markers. We might've been heading south—I couldn't tell for sure. I'd just started to move from "slightly uncomfortable" toward "scared shitless" when I saw a sign for Cranston. I hadn't given much thought about where Shade might live, but I guess it made sense for him to live close to a chapter…so I guessed technically Rebel hadn't lied to me.

We'd have words about this later, I decided. Stern words, and lots of them. Until then, might as well make the most of it. I forced myself to relax, leaning with Shade as we followed the long, sweeping curves of the highway through the hills, arms wrapped tight around his waist.

In a strange way it was almost fun.

Except "fun" wasn't really the right word. Maybe exhilarating, because despite the fact that Shade was scary, he was also sexy in a way I didn't like to think about. (You know, because scary trumps sexy, or it's supposed to.) It was hard to stay scared, though, when we were flying down the road in the darkness, the sound of the big Harley engines surrounding me like a loud but very comfortable blanket.

There was nothing quite like riding a bike at night. One of the things that'd attracted me to Rebel in the first place was his motorcycle. (And yes, I realize that makes me shallow. In my defense, I don't think Rebel even looked up from my boobs to check out my face until our third date, so it wasn't like he was a saint, either.) I'd never ridden before, but from the minute I hopped on the back of his bike, I loved it.

Loved it.

As in, loved everything about it. I loved the wild, free feeling it gave me as the wind blew by. I loved the sound, the sense of connection with the road. I even loved the danger, because the smallest mistake could lead to a crash, yet the man cradled between my thighs was in total control and that was hot.

Unfortunately, riding with Shade was significantly hotter than riding with Rebel. There was something about being so close to him, my front glued to his back as he took full control. The way his body tensed when my fingers gripped him tight. Too, too many tinglies.

This wasn't a good thing.

Not for a girl with a boyfriend. Like I said, I can admit I'm shallow, but I've never been fickle. I wasn't a cheater and something about this seemed like cheating.

Maybe it was the way I could feel all the muscles under his leather.

I mean, I'd speculated when I'd seen him at the barbecue (I'm only human), but until now I hadn't had proof he was actually as sexy under his clothes as my imagination insisted he must be. His thighs were big and solid, too. I knew this because I had to stretch my legs wide to make room for him, and since he didn't have a backrest on the bike, that meant I had to stick tight or risk falling off.

As seductive as all this was, there was also something weirdly relaxing about our ride.

Shade was in charge. Nothing I did could change that, which meant I had to just relax and let him do his thing. When he leaned, I leaned. There was no hope of taking control over the situation, and while riding this fast through the dark should've been scary, he handled the bike in a way that left me feeling completely safe. Rebel was a much sloppier rider. Come to think of it, he was sort of a sloppy lover, too. He made up for it with enthusiasm, but still… I couldn't help but wonder if Shade's control of his bike would extend to other things…

Nope. Don't go there.

Eventually we slowed and I realized we'd come to a town. Cranston, which was bigger than Violetta. A lot bigger. We passed a sign for a University of Idaho satellite campus, and I remembered the catalogue my sister had been looking at last month. She wanted to get a nursing degree, although seeing as she had three little kids and a van that couldn't make it out of the front yard, I wasn't entirely sure it was a realistic goal.

Passing the school, we rode through the small downtown before turning again and heading back out into the countryside. I started to tense up—riding to Cranston was one thing. I hadn't expected to come here, but it also wasn't very far from home. Going past Cranston wasn't part of the deal no matter how you looked at it. I'd just made up my mind to signal Shade to stop when we slowed again, turning onto a gravel road.

The kind of road you drive down to bury bodies.

Rebel, I'm gonna kick your ass for this one.

Thankfully, I saw lights up ahead, and then we pulled up to a building that'd been constructed out of rough-hewn logs. You know, the kind that pioneers used to build because they didn't have any money and that rich people build nowadays because they have too much. At least twenty motorcycles were parked out front, and I saw people on the porch hanging out and drinking beer. Loud music poured out of the building.

I don't know what I'd been expecting, but this wasn't it. Not even a little bit. It couldn't be Shade's home, that was for damned sure. It was a motorcycle clubhouse, and they were in the middle of a full-fledged party. Either Shade had been lying to Rebel or Rebel had been lying to me.

Fucking men.

Shade turned off his motorcycle, and then I was climbing off and hunting for Rebel. He should've been right behind us but there weren't any headlights in the distance. Shade swung off his bike and caught my arm possessively, dragging me toward the broad porch. Something was wrong here. Really wrong. I jerked back against him, but he didn't let go.

"Where's Rebel?" I demanded, a mixture of fear and anger building. Shade might be the club president, but he had no damned right to drag me off like this.

Shitty to be me, because nobody seemed to have told him that.

"Get inside," he said, sounding angry. Really angry. His fingers dug into my arm and I wondered what the hell I'd ever done to him. If Rebel had blown us off, it wasn't exactly my fault. I was just trying to do the two of them a favor.

I stumbled up the steps behind Shade, surrounded by the other bikers who'd been riding with us. Several men on the porch shouted out a welcome, and I saw a woman who looked vaguely familiar frown at me, her expression thoughtful. Then we were through the door and in what would've been a greatroom, if this was a house.

It wasn't a house, though. Not even close.

It didn't have regular furniture, for one thing. Just lots of little tables, a few mismatched couches, two pool tables and a bar along one wall. Across the wall facing the door was a massive Reapers MC sign, complete with the skull and crossed scythes they all wore on the backs of their vests.

Twin blondes wearing nothing but tiny jeans shorts stepped up to Shade. One blocked his path, rubbing her hand down his stomach toward the fly of his pants while the other glared at me.

"You said you'd play with us tonight, Shade," she huffed, boobs jiggling. I stared at them, mesmerized. I mean, they were *right there,* all naked and—

"Change of plans," he replied, and you'd never have guessed a gorgeous, half-naked chick was doing everything in her power to grab his cock. His indifference was chilling. She gave him a sexy little pout—a pout so hot that even I was turned on.

Okay, not really, but you get the picture.

I'd have been all over her if I swung that way.

Instead of responding, Shade grabbed my wrist tighter and pulled me across the room, the crowd parting as more than one biker eyed me curiously. I recognized several more faces from the bar, and a few of the girls smiled at me knowingly.

They definitely had the wrong idea about what was happening here, I realized. Shade hadn't made a secret about his interest in me so I guess it was the logical conclusion, but still…

"Where's Rebel?" I demanded, but either Shade couldn't hear me or he was ignoring me. I had a feeling it was the latter.

Not good.

We passed through the room and into a hallway with bathrooms on either side, then out the back door. There was a covered porch back here, too, full of people smoking. Broad steps led down to a courtyard. In the center was a bonfire. Along the right was a concrete block wall with a covered walkway running alongside. Cleverly hidden speakers played the same music as inside.

I'd never really given much thought to what an MC clubhouse would look like, but this definitely didn't match any of my stereotypes. Under normal circumstances, I'd be full of questions. Tonight, Shade hustled me toward the building on the far side of the courtyard so fast that I could hardly keep up.

This one was long and low and it looked much older. Sort of like a bunkhouse, I decided, with regular windows along the wall. The kind of thing you'd see on a ranch or in a logging camp. The door opened and out stumbled an older man who was clearly drunk, along with a much younger woman who giggled and tugged at her skirt.

Oh, hell no.

This was a bad idea. A very bad idea. I didn't know what was in there for sure, but I'd bet good money it wasn't Rebel with a birthday cake and a bow around his neck.

"I want to go home," I said, jerking back against Shade, trying to stop him. He spun on me, his face dark and intense.

"We'll talk inside," he snarled, then started forward again.

Shit shit shit!

My bunkhouse prediction was right—we passed through the building and turned left, heading down a long hallway with doors on either side at regular intervals. Some were open. I smelled pot in the air. As we walked past one door, I glanced in to find a man I'd seen at the Pit lying back on the bed, smoking a blunt while a blond head bobbed in his lap.

I had no place in my head to store this.

Shade opened a door and pushed me through roughly. I caught a glimpse of a bed before I stumbled. He caught me, kicking the door shut even as he slammed my body against it, covering it with his.

His mouth slanted over mine in the most brutal kiss I'd ever experienced, hands reaching down to grab my thighs, hoisting them up to wrap my legs around his waist.

Chapter Four

My world exploded in a bizarre mix of outrage, fear, confusion and desire. Shade's tongue demanded access to my mouth and I felt his dick between my legs, hard and ready to go. Every nerve in my body screamed at me to do something.

Anything.

My mouth opened to tell him to fuck off and Shade took advantage, thrusting his tongue deep inside. My hands flew up to his hair, my fingers digging deep as I jerked his head back as hard as I could. There was a secret, fucked-up part of me that was turned on by his raw sexuality but I was *not* down with this.

Shade kissed me for a few seconds longer. He could take this as far as he wanted, I realized—no one in this building would lift a finger to stop him.

Holy.

Fucking.

Shit.

I exploded into action, bucking hard as I ripped at his hair. Shade didn't even notice. For an instant, I thought he would go through with it. Then he dropped me, turning away and stalking across the room, punching the wall in sudden fury. Plaster cracked, and he gave a low groan—pain? Frustration? I couldn't tell. Whatever it was, it didn't bode well for Yours Truly. I scrambled to stand as he leaned forward against the shattered wall, then punched it again. *Sweet baby Jesus.* The situation was falling apart fast.

I reached for the doorknob.

"Do *not* open that door," he snarled, and I jumped away like a kid caught trying to steal a cookie. Did the guy have eyes in the back of his head? Shade took a deep, slow breath, then turned back to me, his expression full of dark fire.

"What the fuck's your game?"

"Excuse me?" I replied, astounded.

"Excuse me?" he mocked, his lip curling. "Where the fuck do you think you are, Mandy? This isn't the bar and you aren't gonna get a better tip just 'cause you got a cute ass. You don't fuckin' tease a man like me, and you sure as fuck don't do it in my own Goddamned clubhouse!"

Shade's voice rose as he stalked toward me, all lean strength and grace. Pure predator. I froze, trying to figure out my next move as his words slowly sunk in.

"Wait," I said, raising a hand. He glared at it, and I dropped it back down again, wringing my fingers together nervously. "What are you talking about?"

"You came here of your own free will," Shade snapped. "Don't play stupid."

"I came here to drive Rebel's truck back home for him," I replied, more confused by the minute. "Then you brought me here and dragged me inside. How the hell is that teasing? You scare the shit out of me—I don't even like serving you drinks at the Pit, let alone visiting your stupid clubhouse!"

My voice had grown shrill, the last few words almost a scream.

Shade stilled.

"What did Rebel tell you?" he asked, his voice going so cold that it was almost scarier than when he'd been yelling. Oh my God, he was going to murder me and then my sister wouldn't have anyone to help with the kids and they'd bury me in an unmarked grave and squirrels would eat my eyeballs and—

Mandy! Pull your shit together!

"He told me that he's buying a motorcycle from you," I said

hesitantly. "He wanted to pick it up tonight. He said you were giving him a bargain, and that if he waited you might change your mind. I'm just here to drive the truck back after he gets the bike."

Shade stared at me, his expression unreadable.

"Are you fuckin' stupid?"

"It's not stupid to help out my boyfriend!"

"It is when your boyfriend sets you up. If you were just comin' to pick up a bike, why didn't you ride with him?" Shade asked, the words slow and steady. Like I was a particularly dim child.

Jerkface.

"Because he has a bunch of shit loaded in the truck cab. He didn't come to the bar expecting to buy a bike tonight. He asked me to ride with you because there wasn't room with him."

But as soon as the words were out, I could see his point. Rebel's excuse to get me on Shade's bike was weak. Really weak. But it wasn't like I went around expecting my boyfriend to…do what? Something wrong, but I still had no clue what the hell was really going on here.

"I'm gonna kill him," Shade said slowly, running a hand through his hair. This gave it a sexy, tousled look that would've been very attractive if I hadn't been so busy trying not to pee my pants. "Piece of shit needs to go down."

"I don't understand."

"Rebel traded you to me."

The words were blunt.

Harsh.

Impossible to wrap my head around. I opened my mouth to ask a question, then snapped it shut again because I wasn't even sure what question to ask. I mean, I'd heard what he said, but it didn't make any sense.

"He traded you to me," Shade repeated without a hint of compassion in his eyes. "For the bike. He was short on cash and he knew that I wanted you, so that's what he offered. I asked if you were okay with it and you said yes. So here we are."

"I…" My mouth wouldn't work right. It was like the muscles had gone into shock or something. "H-he *traded* me?"

"Like a baseball card."

Words failed me. *Oh my God. This isn't happening, is it?* Thoughts swirled through my head, along with about a thousand different emotions, but one slowly won out.

Anger.

Raw, unadulterated fury.

Shade wasn't going to kill Rebel. Oh, no. If anyone slit that fucker's throat, it'd be me. But first I'd amputate his balls with a very rusty spoon. Maybe make him eat them.

"What the hell is wrong with you people?" I finally managed to ask. "You can't trade a human being! Rebel's my boyfriend, not my fucking owner! And who the hell accepts a person as a trade for a bike?"

Shade gave me a twisted smile.

"A Reaper."

That sent a chill down my spine because, crazy as it sounded, the man was dead serious.

"In the MC world, you're property," he added bluntly. "How the hell did you spend so much time with his club and not pick up on that?"

This was a good question.

I'd seen the vests some women wore, saying *property of* and their boyfriend's names… It'd always seemed kind of weird. Maybe even cute, in a very politically incorrect way. I hadn't taken it literally, let alone given it serious thought.

Truthfully, I hadn't given much of anything about Rebel a lot of thought.

That'd been one of the chief benefits of having him as a boyfriend, given the train wreck my marriage had been. I didn't have to think about him or worry or plan for the future. We were just having fun together. No stress, no expectations. Just him and me hanging out, riding his bike and occasionally getting drunk and going down on each other. After all the shit I'd gone through with Trevor, I wasn't sure I ever wanted a "real" relationship again.

"Okay," I said, my brain spinning. "Okay, we need to figure this out. Is Rebel coming here?"

"No, he'll pick you up tomorrow, assuming you still want to go with him. And don't worry—he'll show up. No bike until he brings the cash."

"Wait, I thought I *was* the payment."

Shade cocked a brow, a mocking smile twisting his mouth. "It's a three thousand dollar bike. He was short five hundred. You didn't actually think I'd give him a fucking motorcycle worth three grand just to bang his girlfriend, did you?"

I blinked.

What he'd said wasn't exactly flattering, but it was hard to argue. Would I pay three thousand bucks to have sex with someone? Hell, no. Not even David Beckham, and I'd loved him fiercely ever since I'd learned there was a difference between girl parts and boy parts. I shot a glance at Shade, realizing he looked more than a little like Becks, come to think of it. There was just something about him…

No. Just *no.*

"I wouldn't have thought you'd need to pay women to sleep with you," I said, then gave myself a mental kick because that was way too revealing. Shade smiled and took another step toward me. I swallowed. "That came out wrong. I don't suppose there's any chance we can just forget this happened? I mean, obviously I'm going to kill Rebel, but that doesn't really have anything to do with you…"

Well, aside from the fact that he'd been the one on the other end of the trade. Five hundred bucks. I couldn't tell if that was a flattering amount or not.

"I'll take care of Rebel," Shade said, his voice casual but his eyes all business. "If you wanna leave, feel free."

I reached for the door, opening it to find two women making out in the hallway, complete with hands on each other's asses and tongues down each other's throats. A couple of very drunk-looking men watched, one with his hand down his pants. I slammed the door shut and turned to find Shade watching me closely.

"Change your mind?" he asked, cocking a brow. "Not like you're a prisoner here."

Yeah, right. Nobody but Rebel knew where I was. I didn't even have a phone. Even if I made it back through the clubhouse safely, I'd still have to walk miles before I reached town.

"Um, can I borrow your phone? Mine fell in the toilet this morning. I'm pretty sure it's dead."

"No service out here," Shade said, a slow smile spreading over his face. "Of course you could use the landline. Assuming you can find one of the officers and convince him your phone call is more important than whatever—whoever—he's doing."

I closed my eyes, trying to think.

"Will you help me?" I finally asked. Shade shrugged.

"Maybe later," he said. "But right now I'm more interested in gettin' my dick sucked. I was under the impression you had a happy ending for me."

I shivered, torn between disgust and a sick curiosity about what a happy ending with Shade would feel like. God knew I wouldn't be having any happy endings with Rebel any time soon—whatever else came out of tonight, our relationship was over.

Now what?

"Tell you what," Shade said slowly. "I'll make you a deal."

I didn't want to trust him, but it wasn't like I had a lot of choices here. "I'm listening…"

"We'll compromise," he continued. "Tonight didn't go right for either of us. Let's have a drink and relax for a while, then I'll go find someone to suck my dick and you can crash here. You'll be fine. Not a man in this building is stupid enough to fuck with my woman."

"I'm not your woman," I insisted quickly, and he cocked that brow again.

"You're in my room and you're gonna sleep in my bed tonight. You're under my protection. Makes you my woman, at least in their eyes. That means nobody'll touch you without my permission, and tomorrow I'll take you home, safe and sound."

"And what do you get out of this?" I asked, suspicious. Shade turned away, walking over to a dresser I hadn't noticed before. On the top was a bottle of what looked like whiskey, along with some plastic cups.

"I'm not getting jack shit," he said, opening the bottle and pouring a drink. "Which is why you should take me up on it before I change my mind. You wanna be pissed at someone, save it for your loser boyfriend."

He filled the second cup, then turned to me, holding it out. I considered, wondering if he was planning to drug me or something. God, how had I gotten into this?

How many times do you have to get screwed over before you learn, Mandy?

"What, you scared I'm gonna roofie you?" Shade asked. The words were ugly but he seemed more amused than anything. "Sorry to disappoint you, sweetheart, but you aren't worth a felony. I mean, you got a nice ass, but life is too fuckin' short to spend it in jail. Not only that, unlike your boyfriend, I'm not a fuckin' liar. I'm gonna do something to you, I'll tell you because I'm not a little bitch."

While I wasn't a huge fan of the "little bitch" reference, I had to admit it summed up my feelings toward Rebel pretty well. And a drink really would be good… I reached for the cup, knocking it back quickly. Its smooth burn startled me because it was good—really good. Whiskey wasn't my favorite, but I'd served enough of it to know this wasn't the cheap-ass shit Bone kept on the bottom shelf. Shade gave a low laugh, knocking back his own shot. I felt the alcohol warm me as he refilled the glasses. Drinking any more was probably a bad idea, but I could probably sip at it without getting wasted.

There's a time and a place for liquid courage.

Shade turned and sat down on the bed, leaning against the backboard. He took another swallow of whiskey while I searched for a place to sit. My options were the bed or the floor, so I leaned back against the door instead.

"So…" I said, wondering what the hell to talk about. Shade eyed me, and while there was still heat in his gaze, I wasn't getting the same sense of threat from him. He'd relaxed, I realized. He really wasn't coming after me.

Disappointed? I asked myself. *Don't be a moron. This is a gift. Take it.*

Maybe Shade and I could become friends and he'd help me hide Rebel's body. *He probably knows all the best ways to kill someone without making a mess.*

This was the kind of information I needed.

"What the hell are you doing with a piece of shit like Rebel?" Shade asked, raising one of his legs and resting the arm holding the glass across his knee. The fabric of his jeans pulled tight between his legs and—

I looked away, suddenly fascinated by the hole where he'd punched the wall.

"You gonna answer the question?" Shade asked, sounding amused. I glanced back toward him.

"I don't suppose you'd believe we're soul mates," I said, taking a sip of my drink. Damn, that was really smooth. Shade cocked a brow and laughed.

"No, probably not. Seriously—why the hell are you with him? Rebel's a piece of shit."

"He's cute," I said, flushing because the answer was so stupid. "I'm shallow, all right? And he's fun. I never thought there was any potential for a future there, but that's not what I'm looking for. I just wanted someone to hang out with. And…okay, this part is really embarrassing."

I shot another look at him. Shade waited patiently. No pressure. I felt myself relaxing more.

"I thought he was sexy on his bike," I admitted. "He asked me out and we had fun. I started hanging around with his riding club a lot, and I liked them, too. That's how I got the job at the Pit."

"You know he's cheating on you, right?" Shade asked casually. My stomach clenched, although I didn't know why. I'd suspected it already, and considering the guy had tried to trade me for a motorcycle, it wasn't like I had any illusions that he was a keeper.

"Let's talk about something else."

"Sure," Shade said. "You're new to the area. How'd you end up in Violetta?"

"How do you know I'm new?" I asked, startled.

"Because I made it my business to know," he replied. "Hand me the bottle."

I stepped over to the dresser and grabbed it, walking hesitantly toward the bed. I expected him to take it but he held out his glass instead. Pouring carefully, I gave him a refill.

"You can sit down," he said, glancing toward the empty space beside him. "If I was going to pull something, I would've by now."

"You sure you aren't just trying to get me drunk so I'll have sex with you?" I asked. Then I gave myself a mental kick, because that's the kind of thing you think, not the kind of thing you say. Shade burst out laughing and for once the sound wasn't mocking.

"Of course I'm trying to get you drunk," he said. "I want to fuck you—this isn't a secret. But I'm also not a fuckin' rapist—think we covered that already—so all you have to do is say no and you'll be fine. In the meantime, you might as well take a break, because I'm not getting up and you're gonna get tired of standing eventually."

I *was* tired, actually, and my feet hurt. They always did after a shift at the bar. The bed looked comfortable enough and mostly clean. Not only that, Shade genuinely wasn't putting any moves on me. He seemed to be relaxed and enjoying his drink.

"Okay," I said, expecting him to scoot over and make room.

"You wanna climb over me or use those legs of yours to walk around to the other side?" he asked, sounding amused. "I'm not moving my ass just so you can steal the warm spot."

"You sure aren't…"

Shade's mouth quirked. "Aren't what?"

"Aren't trying very hard to get me into bed," I said. A giggle broke free and I felt my cheeks warm. Shade shrugged.

"We covered this. Now you sitting your ass down or not? I want another drink, so hand that bottle over."

"You're full of shit!" I said, waving my hand grandly. My drink sloshed and I licked the side of the cup, because this whiskey was way too good to waste even a single drop. "Wonder Woman is better than Batman. She's got *real* power, not just fancy toys. Although she has those, too, which means anything Batman can do, she can do better."

"Nope," Shade said, shaking his head seriously. "She's hot, I'll give her that, but he'd take her in a fair fight."

I held up a hand for him to wait as I polished off my booze.

"No way. She's a *goddess of war* and she's one of the best hand-to-hand fighters in history. She's got an invisible jet, for God's sake. How can you compete with that? All he has is a bunch of money and the stupid Batmobile."

"Hand over the cup," Shade said, narrowing his eyes.

"Why?" I asked, narrowing mine right back. I was good and drunk now, and I wasn't sure I was ready to be done for the night.

"Demonstration," he replied. "C'mon. Or are you chicken?"

"What are we, kindergartners?"

"You're the one insisting Wonder Woman can take Batman," he replied. *"Chicken."*

Then he leaned toward me, raising a single finger to poke me in the center of my chest. Not copping a feel or anything remotely sexual, either. This was pure taunt. I handed him the cup and he tossed it on the floor, nearly falling off the bed in the process. I smirked—guess I wasn't the only drunk one. Then he started listing to the side and I lunged for him, grabbing his shirt to keep him from going over.

Shade caught my arm, using the momentum to pull me onto his body with sudden force. My hands hit his chest and I raised my head to stare at him, stunned.

"What the hell are you doing?" I asked. Shade wrapped his arms around my waist, holding me tight to his body.

"Demonstrating."

I frowned, trying to figure it out, and then he rolled over, pinning me with his body. One of his knees came down between my thighs, spreading my legs. My hands were trapped tight against his chest, our faces inches apart. My head spun from the booze and as he grinned at me, I realized I'd made a very serious mistake.

Shade was nowhere near as drunk as me.

Not even close.

"Batman will always win," he said, giving me that same predatory look that'd scared the crap out of me earlier. It still scared me a little, but it was exciting, too. I could smell him, all leather and whiskey and pure sex. There was something about being held down like this…like I could just relax and let it happen, without having to take responsibility for it.

Shut the fuck up, Mandy. You think Wonder Woman would settle for this?

She really wouldn't.

"You should let me go," I told Shade, my voice firm.

"Admit that Batman would beat Wonder Woman and I will," he said, his voice penetrating the fog clogging my mind. "He's stronger and he can hold his liquor better. It's basic physics. Throw in some chemistry with all that body mass and Wonder Woman doesn't have a chance."

"Fuck you," I whispered, mesmerized. There were tingles rushing through me and my head was spinning. All I could see were his eyes, dark and pulsing with something that had absolutely nothing to do with the relative fighting strengths of superheroes.

"You can fuck me any time you want, baby," he said. The words were low, grating with a need so intense I clenched my thighs. *Stop this. Stop it right now or you'll let him do it.* I lunged toward him with my teeth and he laughed, pinning me with his hips, his cock rock hard against my stomach.

"You can't win," Shade taunted. "I'm stronger than you."

"I thought this was about superheroes," I managed to say, shoving at his chest. He reached between us, grabbing my wrists and pinning them over my head one at a time, until both were held tight in one strong hand.

"What are we, in kindergarten?" he asked, repeating my own words mockingly. Then he ground his hips into mine. The weight of his body pulled down the neck of my shirt and I knew all sorts of cleavage was on display.

You can use this, my inner Wonder Woman whispered. *Take back control. Do it for me and Hippolyta and all the other Amazons. Teach him a lesson.* I wished I could but he had a point with the whole physics thing.

I've never even owned a magic lasso, I told her mournfully.

The sexy bastard causing all my trouble stayed silent, waiting me out.

"One kiss," I said finally, glaring. Shade smiled.

"One kiss in exchange for what?"

"Letting me go."

"I can just take a kiss and keep you here," he said. "New deal. One kiss and you admit Wonder Woman would lose. Then I'll let you go."

"Absolutely not. No kiss, no admission," I countered. "In exchange, you let me go and I won't press charges for assault."

Shade burst out laughing. "Pretty ballsy for someone stuck in the middle of a Reapers' clubhouse without a cell phone or a ride home."

He made a good point.

Think about what I'd do in this situation, Wonder Woman said firmly. *Are you really going to let this biker win? Kick his ass!*

Unfortunately, my best thinking parts were all drunk, which meant that the non-thinking parts—specifically those between my legs—were taking over fast. They sort of liked the idea of Batman in charge, and Shade was already dressed in black and everything. *Behave,* I instructed them firmly.

"One kiss with tongue," I countered. "I won't give up Wonder Woman, but I won't press charges, either."

"One kiss with tongue," he replied, eyes darkening. "And you sleep with me tonight. I don't really give a fuck about Wonder Woman."

"Sleep with you?" I hissed. "Oh, hell no. I'm not that drunk."

"Not sex. Just sleep. Right here in this bed, with me. All night."

"No sex."

"No sex unless you want it," he said, and my breath caught because I sort of did want it.

"All right," I replied. When his head lowered toward mine I could hardly breathe, I was so excited. His last kiss had been rough, almost brutal. Now his lips were soft, nipping and nibbling at mine. I opened for him, expecting the kiss to deepen. Instead he touched the corner of my mouth, rubbing his nose alongside mine before drifting down along my jawline.

When his mouth found the spot right below my ear I nearly called bullshit, but it felt so good. Warm tingles ran through my stomach and my nipples hardened. Shade slid down a few inches, pushing my knees apart with his as he settled more firmly between my legs, my hands still held prisoner over my head. His cock pushed directly against my center. I sighed.

This was good. Really good.

Then he caught my earlobe between his lips and my head spun, a mixture of lust and booze making it almost impossible to think.

Almost.

But not quite.

This was happening, I realized. I was actually going to have sex with this man unless I did something to stop it right now because he wanted me. Bad. I wanted him, too, and despite the fact that I hadn't officially broken up with Rebel yet, that relationship was definitely over.

Would it really be such a horrible idea to sleep with him?

He gave Rebel a $500 discount off a bike to fuck you, Wonder Woman reminded me coldly. *And he thinks Batman could beat me and we both know that's bullshit. Are you a goddess of war or not?*

Shade's tongue slid into my mouth as his hand caught the edge of my shirt, tugging it upward. My head spun because he tasted amazing. Whiskey and smoke and sex and…five hundred dollars to fuck me.

Shut it down, Wonder Woman demanded. *You have sex with him tonight and you're officially a prostitute. A* cheap *prostitute. You think I'd fuck Batman for anything less than ten grand?*

Damn it, she was right. I twisted my head, breaking the kiss. Shade followed, trying to catch my lips. I caught his with my teeth instead, biting him hard enough to draw blood. His head jerked back and he stared down at me, panting.

"You want this as bad as I do."

"I said one kiss. It's over," I insisted, wishing my voice wasn't so breathless and eager. "Don't make me bite you again."

Shade closed his eyes, inhaling slowly. His cock pulsed against me and it took everything I had not to grind up against him.

"Fucking hell," he muttered, opening his eyes again. "Jesus *Christ* but you're a fucking tease."

"I am not. The agreement was one kiss with tongue."

Wonder Woman nodded proudly.

Shade rolled off, sitting up on the bed to face away from me, running a hand through his hair.

"I need to get the fuck outta here," he snapped. Then he stood and made for the door.

"Wait!" I said, reality crushing down around me. I couldn't have sex with him but that didn't change the situation—I was alone in the Reapers' clubhouse, completely at the club's mercy. "Am I still safe here?"

Shade turned on me, two hundred pounds plus of pissed-off male, and I scrambled back against the wall behind the bed.

The same wall he'd punched a hole through with his bare hand.

"Yeah, you're safe," he said coldly. "Not gonna rape you, Mandy. Not gonna roofie you. Not gonna murder you or tie you to the bed or even fucking kiss you again unless you ask, because unlike your piece of shit boyfriend, I'm a real man and I don't fucking abuse women. You win. I'll give you a ride home tomorrow and you'll never have to see me again. Happy?"

He turned away without waiting for an answer, slamming the door behind him as he left the room. This left me alone to gloat over my victory. He was right—I'd won. A full-on triumph for me and Wonder Woman. Somehow it just didn't quite feel like one, though.

I'm also kind of lonely, she admitted.

Fucking bitch.

She could've mentioned that earlier.

Chapter Five

My head throbbed as I stared up at an unfamiliar ceiling.

What the hell?

A thick, muscular arm shifted under me, tucking me into a man's torso. My head rested against him like a pillow. Too muscular to be Rebel, and he didn't smell quite right. Not bad, just…different.

Shade.

The night came back in a rush, everything from what Rebel had done to how the big Reaper's kiss had turned me inside out. Wonder Woman was mixed up in there somehow, but I couldn't quite remember how. *Nothing weird about that.* At any rate, Shade had left after I turned him down, but not before promising that I'd be safe. And I had been. I'd sat and stewed for a while, then awarded myself another drink and passed out.

Sometime in the night, he must've come back.

Shouldn't have had so much booze, I thought, blinking at the harsh sunlight. Wait. Sunlight. It was morning, which meant my sister would be headed to work soon.

I needed to get my ass home in time to watch the kids…unless it was too late already.

Shit.

There wasn't a clock in the room, or a phone. I needed to call her ASAP and let her know I hadn't flaked, except I sort of *had* flaked. Not on purpose, though.

Fucking Rebel, setting me up and then leaving me stranded here.

Something stirred against my leg, which was draped over Shade's body. Some of his parts were less asleep than others, because that was some impressive morning wood poking my thigh. He'd promised to give me a ride in the morning.

This wasn't the kind of ride I'd been thinking of.

Might be a good idea to find a phone before waking him up. Maybe pull myself together and figure out a plan so that my sister didn't end up having to choose between her kids and her job. Goddamn men. None of this would've happened if we'd stayed single.

If there was one thing we should've learned by now, it was that McBride women couldn't pick men for shit. Our mom had been married five times, and not one of them had been worth keeping. Both Hannah and I had struck out, too, although at least I hadn't gotten left to raise three kids by myself. Not that I'd trade my little nieces for anything on earth, but still… Men hadn't exactly been a force for good in our lives.

So. First thing—find a phone and call Hannah. Then figure out how to get home. Shade had promised me a lift, but I didn't want to wake him up. Not yet. Not in bed with a stiffy of that magnitude.

Sliding out from under his arm very carefully, I dropped my feet to the floor and grabbed my bag. The room looked smaller in the daylight. Dingier, too. Shade might have a few things thrown around, but it obviously wasn't a full-time home. More of a place to crash. Reminded me of my corner of the bedroom at Hannah's place. Her ex's parents had let her stay in the little trailer that she'd shared with Randy rent free, but there wasn't a hell of a lot of extra room. I kept my stuff in a suitcase and slept on the couch most nights. She insisted we could share the bed, but there was almost always at least one kid in there with us. Nothing quite like three-year-old twins kicking your kidneys to keep you awake and alert all night long.

The couch was a lot more restful.

Easing open the door, I started down the deserted hallway. There had to be a phone around here somewhere, right? Most of the doors were closed, although a couple had been left open. I glanced in one to find the two girls from the hall last night buck naked on a bed with a biker I'd never seen before.

Damn.

Those girls got around.

I reached the end of the bunkhouse and let myself out into the courtyard, which was full of debris from the party. The fire pit gave off an anemic trail of smoke. Red cups littered the ground, and toward the back I spotted three little tents. Guess they'd had company from out of town. This probably held some significance, but damned if I knew what it might be. The back door of the clubhouse was unlocked, so I let myself in and headed toward the main room, where I finally found signs of life.

Specifically, there was a girl about my age wandering around, picking up garbage and throwing it into a white plastic kitchen bag.

"Grab the broom, will you? And the dustpan. There's a broken bottle back here," she said without looking at me. I glanced around, wondering where the broom might be.

"Hey—who the hell are you?" asked someone else, and I looked up to find one of the guys, a younger one who didn't have a Reaper's vest, stepping through a side door. The girl spun around and raised her eyebrows, clearly startled.

"I'm sorry," she said. "I thought it was Samantha. She must be back in the kitchen."

"You didn't answer the question," he told me, ignoring the girl. "You look familiar. Where do I know you from?"

"I'm Mandy McBride," I said, swallowing uncomfortably. "I work at the Pit. Waitress."

"You're the waitress?" the girl asked, looking me over with a critical eye. "I heard all about you last night. Shade know you're leaving?"

"Shade's asleep," I said. "I just need to use a phone. I'm supposed to be watching my sister's kids this morning while she works. Do you have any idea what time it is?"

"It's about seven," the girl replied slowly. "And there's a phone on the wall. But I think you should check with Shade before you do anything. He might have plans—"

I was already grabbing the phone, a battered, old-fashioned beast with a long, coiled cord. Couldn't remember the last time I'd seen anything like it, but it worked.

"Hello," said a small, soft voice. My five-year-old niece, Callie, had answered. Knowing my luck, Hannah was in the shower.

"Hey baby," I replied, careful not to let any of my frustration into my voice. "This is Auntie Mandy. Is Mommy around?"

"She's sleeping."

"Can you go wake her up?"

"She said to be quiet. Her head hurts."

Oh, shit. Hannah had gotten migraines ever since she was a little girl. Not sort-of-uncomfortable-but-manageable-with-Tylenol migraines, but full-on, knock-you-on-your-ass-after-hallucinating-and-puking-for-hours migraines.

"Have you had any breakfast?" I asked, trying not to panic. Callie was the oldest. She could help the twins get some cereal, maybe turn on the TV until I got home. It was either that or call Randy, and he was worse than useless. Hannah had finally kicked his sorry ass out when she learned he'd been selling drugs while he was supposed to be watching the kids.

His parents were theoretically willing to help, but his dad was stuck in a wheelchair and his mom was legally blind. Thus the need for my relocation…

"Yeah, we ate some Cheerios and a candy bar," Callie said proudly. "I cooked it in the microwave and it was soft and yummy. The twins want to go outside and play in the dirt. I told them Mommy wouldn't like that."

"You're right—definitely stay inside," I replied, thinking fast. "Turn on the TV, but keep it quiet so it doesn't hurt Mommy's head. I'll get home as fast as I can. Until then, don't bother Mommy unless it's an emergency. You remember what an emergency is?"

"Yes," she said gravely. "If there's blood or someone can't breathe or there's a fire."

"And do you open the door?"

"Only to a firefighter or the police. Not for Daddy, even if he's being nice."

My heart caught, because it wasn't fair that a kid so young should have to deal with shit like this.

"All right, then," I told her, forcing myself to take a deep breath. "You're doing great. I'll get home as fast as I can. You watch your sisters until then."

"I'm a big girl. I can do it."

I hung up the phone, running a hand through my hair, my own headache growing steadily worse. I felt like I should call someone, but who? The girls were safe and the last thing Hannah needed was an investigation from CPS. Given the whole single-mom thing—combined with the fact that she was an outsider and their dad was the local drug dealer—she didn't look so good on paper. But she was a good mom. A *really* good mom.

Just get your ass back to the trailer and things will be fine.

But how was I going to do that?

"Everything all right?" the girl asked, looking concerned. She had big raccoon eyes from smears of makeup and was still wearing a teeny tank top with a push-up bra from the night before, but a sort of innate kindness still shined through.

"Not really," I admitted. "I need to get back home."

"Where's home?"

"Violetta."

"You shouldn't leave without talking to Shade first," the guy said, and his voice was firm. His hair was all flattened on one side where he'd passed out—probably on one of the couches lining the room—but despite the silly hair, I didn't want to mess with him.

"He said he'd give me a ride—" I told him. Then someone started pounding on the main door, startling the hell out of me. Instantly three men I hadn't noticed (had they been sleeping on the couches?) were on their feet, one of them looking through the peephole while another stood ready by the door.

"It's that tool, Rebel," one of them said, glancing toward me. "He's your boyfriend, right?"

Damn, gossip spread fast in this place.

"Ex-boyfriend," I said grimly. My fury from the night before came rushing back, mixing with my worry about the girls and the pain of my headache to create a roar in my ears. I couldn't fix things for my sister. I had no clue how I was going to get home and I still couldn't quite wrap my head around what'd happened, but one thing was very clear in my mind.

Rebel needed his ass kicked, and I was just the girl to do it.

Chapter Six

Shade

"Boss, we got a situation with your girl."

I woke instantly, reaching for the gun I kept under the bed as I rolled to my feet. It was an old habit, one that'd scared the shit out of more than one woman, but it'd served me well during my years as a club enforcer.

Nowadays, I always traveled with security—one of the many "perks" of being national president. Got on my nerves in a big way. I also understood the reasoning behind it. Nothing throws a club into chaos like seeing their president gunned down, or worse, taken hostage. Not that the brothers would be stupid enough to give in to any demands if it happened, but they'd kill themselves trying to rescue me. Taking on the job meant losing some freedom, which sucked.

"What's the problem?" I asked, although I had a pretty good idea already. Mandy was gone, and seeing as she had no transportation, that meant she had to be wandering around the clubhouse. Nobody would give her a ride without my permission.

Fucking hell, but that bitch had me tied in knots.

Why I gave a shit about her I had no fuckin' idea, but I knew one thing for sure—I wouldn't be happy until I was balls deep in that sweet snatch of hers. Fuckin' hated watching the eyes that followed her at the bar. Every man in the place wanted a piece of that. I hated them all, but I hated Rebel more than the rest combined because at the end of the day, he was the one hitting that.

He'd been mouthing off last night about how tight her asshole was, and when he'd offered her to me, I'd known it was a bad idea to say yes… But I wanted her. Wanted her bad. Bad enough to drag her back to the clubhouse, despite the fact that I knew it wouldn't end well.

Every second of the ride had been hell. Half of me wanted to howl at the moon in triumph because I was finally gonna fuck this woman who'd been driving me crazy. The other half wanted to kill someone, because apparently she loved that fuckwit loser so much that she'd pimp herself out for him.

By the end of the night my balls were blue and I'd been frustrated as hell, but there'd been relief, too. I'd seen the fury in her eyes when she'd realized what he'd done.

Fuckin' gorgeous, that.

"Rebel's out in front of the clubhouse," said McClane. He was a local brother who'd been assigned to help me out as needed, and the man was damned good at his job. "Your girl's about to kill him with her bare hands. Wonderin' if you want us to step in?"

His face was carefully blank, but I saw the hint of humor in his eyes.

"You're enjoying this, aren't you?" I asked, reaching for my boots.

"It's pretty funny," he said, studying me. "You fuck her last night?"

"Nope."

He smiled. "So she's not a whore?"

"Not Rebel's whore, anyway," I said, holding back my own grin. "Who's out there with her?"

"Half the clubhouse," he replied. "Everyone's waiting for you. Not club business, but we don't want your woman gettin' fucked up, either."

"Appreciate that."

He shrugged, slapping me on the back as I passed through the door. Whatever else happened, watching Mandy take on Rebel should be entertaining.

Mandy

"You Goddamn piece of shit!" I hissed, stalking toward my future ex-boyfriend. I couldn't believe the fuckwit had the nerve to show his face… Although I wasn't stupid enough to think he was here for me. Nope. He'd come to collect his bike. The bastard held up his hands, giving me that cute little puppy dog face I used to think was so adorable.

Yeah. Not so fucking cute any more.

"It's not like you got hurt," he said, his voice wheedling. "And you're always saying you want to help me get ahead. I couldn't have pulled this off without you, and it didn't even cost you anything. And just think—now we can start riding together again. I know how much you've missed riding!"

I felt my blood pressure rise. All my life I'd been surrounded by people who thought I was trashy, but I'd taken great pride in the fact that I never acted that way. I wasn't the type to scream at people in public, I didn't air my dirty laundry and I never, ever put on a show for anyone. I'd survived twenty-seven years, five step-dads and one failed marriage without losing my dignity, but this was the end.

"You treated me like a fucking whore!" I screamed, then balled up my fist and punched him in the stomach as hard as I could, savoring the look of utter shock on his face. Then that same face transformed into something ugly as he caught me by the shoulders and threw me into his truck.

I hit *hard* and stumbled, falling to the side and clipping the mirror with my cheek on the way down.

Black swirled behind my eyes. I blinked, trying to catch my breath as my face throbbed in time to my heartbeat. Rebel gave a startled squeal as one of the Reapers—Dopey, the anti-dwarf I'd met last night—knocked his head back with a crack. My ex-boyfriend hit the ground and Dopey kicked him in the side for good measure.

Rebel moaned.

"Touching her was stupid," the big man said. "Now Shade's gonna be in a bad mood and that won't end well."

I took a deep breath, looking around to find half the clubhouse watching our little scene. My back hurt and my cheek throbbed where it'd hit the truck's side mirror. I reached up, touching it carefully as I considered my options.

"Shade's coming!" one of the girls said breathlessly. Rebel tried to push himself up, his face filling with panic. Another biker stepped forward, raising a baseball bat.

Holy shit.

This was actually happening. *This is my life.* I was really surrounded by angry Reapers and their women, and my ex was gonna get *destroyed.* I might be new to the area, but I'd been around long enough to know how things worked around here—these guys could do whatever the hell they wanted without any consequences.

A good girl would be scared.

A decent girl would find a way to run.

I'd been a good girl for most of my life, though, and what'd it gotten me? A couch in a trailer and a boyfriend who traded me for a fucking motorcycle. *He only traded you for* part *of a fucking motorcycle,* Wonder Woman whispered in my ear.

Too true, sister. Too true.

"Give me the bat," I said, my voice cold and strong. The bikers glanced at each other, and Dopey shrugged. His fellow Reaper tossed me the bat and I caught it like a badass, hefting it thoughtfully in my hands. A flash of sunlight reflected in the truck's side mirror caught my eye, reminding me that I'd have one hell of a bruise soon. I raised the bat, took aim and hit the mirror so hard it went flying.

"Fuck!" someone shouted, but I didn't pay attention. Rebel loved that truck. Not as much as he'd loved his motorcycle, but enough that destroying it would hit him hard. Raising the bat again, I circled the vehicle, then aimed for a headlight, smashing that out too. Oh, this was good. Very therapeutic. Whoops and cheers went up around me as I took out another light, the other mirror and then attacked the windshield. The glass cracked but it didn't break, which was frustrating as hell. I'd just turned the bat around to use as a battering ram when someone grabbed me around the waist, pulling me back and away.

"You need to stop," Shade told me, his voice in my ear low and controlled.

"No," I snarled, bucking against him. "I want to kill him and kill his truck and cut off his balls and—"

"And you can," he said soothingly. "But this isn't the right way to do it. You're gonna hurt yourself if you don't calm down."

The adrenaline surging through my body begged to differ, but he held me tight, forcing me to settle. I considered fighting him but that wouldn't do any good. He'd made his point last night—Batman was stronger than Wonder Woman.

Fucking stupid men.

I stilled and Shade let me go, reaching out for the bat. I stared down at his hand, hating the fact that yet another man was telling me what to do. His club surrounded me, though. They had all the power.

Men *always* had all the power.

I forced my fingers to release my weapon. Shade smiled at me, tossing it to the ground. Then he raised his other arm, offering me something.

A tire iron.

"This'll do a lot more damage," Shade said, the words just for me. "You fuck up his truck as much as you want, but don't touch him. Not here. We'll take care of him later when there aren't so many witnesses."

My mouth gaped. "Are you serious?"

"Always," he replied, reaching out to touch the tip of my nose. "That was cute with the bat, but show me what you can do with a tire iron, baby."

I grinned like a lunatic, wrapping my fingers around the heavy bar and turning toward the truck again, taking careful aim. The metal hit the windshield with a shattering crash, the curved tip finally punching through the weak spot. The safety glass didn't totally disintegrate but it'd still cost a fortune to replace, and I knew for a fact Rebel didn't have any insurance.

Yeah, I had real a gift for picking winners.

I smashed the windshield again, then went after the driver's side window. It wasn't enough, though. I wanted more. Circling, I studied the truck and then glanced down at Rebel, who still cowered on the ground. He watched me with wide, terrified eyes, and I let my gaze fall to his crotch. Trade me like a baseball card, would he?

God, but I'd love to take that tire iron to his balls.

Shade was right, though. There were a lot of witnesses and I didn't want to go back to jail. Ever. That didn't mean I couldn't fuck with Rebel's head a little, though.

"Do you have a knife I can borrow?" I asked Shade. He raised a brow, then glanced toward Dopey. The man shrugged and unsnapped the leather strap that held a large knife sheathed to his leg. He handed it to me wordlessly. I tested the sharpness against my thumb, the thinnest of blood lines welling up from the tiny cut. It hurt, but not half as bad as Rebel had hurt me.

"I should cut off your balls," I told my former boyfriend. "You tricked me and tried to use me like a whore. Now you're going to pay for that."

Rebel moaned in terror as I stepped toward him, sending a thrill through me. *Damned straight you should be afraid, motherfucker.* Then I turned away, smiling as I drove the knife deep into one of his tires. The air rushed out. I moved on to the next, and the next. By the fourth I felt some of my adrenaline fading. Rebel was sobbing, and all around me bikers were laughing and clapping. I turned to Dopey, carefully rotating the knife to offer him the handle.

"Thank you."

Then I took a deep breath, wiping my forehead. Goddamn, but it was a beautiful morning.

Shade stepped up to me, looking almost proud. Something sparked between us, something wild and fun and free. Something close to the feeling I got from riding on the back of a motorcycle, a mixture of thrill and excitement and sheer joy as the wind tore through my hair and sang in my ear.

"That was the sexiest fuckin' thing I've ever seen," Shade said. He caught the back of my head in his big hand, pulling me in hard for a kiss. His other arm wrapped around my body, holding me tight as his tongue ravaged my mouth like it belonged to him. God help me, in that moment it did. My body went molten, the thrill turning to something else—something more intense—as his tongue thrust deep.

I wanted to stay here, I realized. Let him drag me back into his clubhouse to his ratty old bed, rip off my clothes and fuck me until I forgot reality. The past few months had been tough, and while I'd had fun with Rebel, I'd never really been able to count on him. I had a feeling that if I just did what Shade wanted—*followed* him like a good biker babe—he'd take care of everything and I wouldn't have to think for a while or make any tough decisions.

God, but I wanted that.

Unfortunately, the only thing my niece Callie knew how to cook was chocolate. There were three little girls waiting for me, along with a sister who was probably in agony and almost certainly at risk of losing her job for missing yet another day of work. Pulling away from that kiss was one of the hardest things I've ever done, but I managed somehow. Shade's eyes were dark and hungry. Full of fire. For once that didn't scare me.

"I need to go home," I whispered. "My sister is sick and I've got to watch the kids. Will you give me a ride?"

Shade met my gaze steadily.

"This isn't over," he said, and he wasn't talking about the situation with Rebel.

"My oldest niece is only five, and she already microwaved them a candy bar for breakfast."

Shade cocked his head at me. "No shit?"

"No shit," I replied solemnly.

"Then I guess I'd better give you a ride," he said slowly. He glanced toward Rebel and his face hardened. "Get in your truck and go away."

Rebel looked to the truck, almost comical in his confusion. "But the tires are all flat."

"So drive on the rims," Shade told him. "Make yourself disappear or I'll do it for you."

Rebel nodded quickly. I watched while he staggered to his feet, clutching his side as he lurched toward the Chevy. Then Shade caught my hand, tugging me toward the line of bikes. I turned toward him and he froze, reaching up to touch the side of my face.

"You've got a bruise starting here. Rebel hit you," he said, his voice like ice. I shook my head.

"Technically, he threw me into the truck."

Shade's face went hard. "I'm gonna kill him."

"No," I said, catching his arm. "You're gonna give me a ride home. I don't care about that fucker, but I do care about my nieces. If you want to help me, take me home."

Shade turned to Dopey, who stood watching Rebel. "Follow him."

Dopey nodded sharply and a chill ran down my spine, because as much as I hated Rebel, I had a bad feeling about this—if Shade wanted to throw him into a truck, I was totally down with that. The whole disappearing thing, though… That sounded like some seriously bad karma.

"Shade—"

"Rebel's not your problem anymore," he said, glancing down at me. "He touched what was mine on my property. That's a problem between him and me."

I opened my mouth to argue, then closed it again because he'd gone back to scaring me, way beyond Batman level. Rebel was a piece of shit, but Shade was a whole different level of badass. I'd gotten so caught up in his kiss that I'd forgotten how dangerous he was.

Big mistake.

I needed to get home and get away from him. Maybe find a new job where I wouldn't have to see him again. I didn't care how sexy he was—I'd had enough dangerous men to last me a lifetime.

Chapter Seven

The ride home was anti-climactic.

Last night it'd felt like Shade was kidnapping me away to another world. In the daylight, I recognized the highway curving around rolling hills and clumps of forest. The same mountains that I saw above Hannah's trailer stood over us, watching.

Just like our first trip together, I held Shade tightly around the waist, taking in his special scent and feeling the play of his stomach muscles under my hands. Everything about him felt sexy and right, scarily enough. I refused to relax into him, though, because I couldn't afford that. When I'd met Rebel, I'd decided it was safe to have a boyfriend so long as I didn't trust him with my heart.

Now I knew better.

By the time we pulled up in front of the trailer I shared with my sister's family—and Shade knew exactly where it was, which was a little creepy in and of itself—I was utterly resolved. Whatever chemistry we might have, I wasn't interested in acting on it. Self-preservation and all that.

That didn't stop the strange twinge I felt, seeing the place as it must look through his eyes. Our home was quite literally on the wrong side of the tracks. Violetta only had nine hundred residents, with the poorest ten percent living on the flat behind the old grain elevator and rail yard.

My sister's battered old minivan sat up on blocks and the trailer itself was frayed and stained from too many winters. A cheap swing set sat in the tiny yard, which was well-maintained because my sister took the whole mothering thing very seriously. She didn't want the girls stepping on any rusty nails.

Two more Reapers—including Dopey—had followed us from the clubhouse. Shade gave them a wave and they passed, circling around the block as he pulled his Harley to a stop in the driveway. He turned off the big engine and my entire body quivered from a mixture of phantom vibrations and suppressed tension. I climbed down, determined to head off any ideas he might have about following me inside.

"You working at the Pit again tonight?" he asked, reaching up to touch my cheek. His touch was gentle, but it still hurt. I ignored his question.

"Don't do anything to Rebel," I told him seriously. "If you do, the cops will come talk to me, and the last thing I need is more cops in my life."

"Whatever business Rebel has with the Reapers, it won't roll over on you," Shade said. "I wouldn't put you in that position. You didn't answer my question, though. You workin' tonight?"

"Yeah, but I'm going to ask Bone to have someone else wait on the Reapers in the future. I'm out, Shade. I don't want to be part of your world."

Shade's eyes narrowed.

"This thing between us isn't over," he said firmly.

"It is to me," I replied, ignoring the way his hand had slipped into the hair at the back of my neck. I wanted to lean into him and purr like a cat. A very stupid cat. "There's nowhere we can go with this personally. And the last time I served you at the Pit I busted ass all night and didn't even get a tip. So far as I'm concerned, it's a dead end."

Shade cocked his head and smirked. "So I was supposed to tip you on top of the five hundred I gave Rebel to fuck you?"

"I never agreed to that," I reminded him.

"Yeah, you made that pretty clear."

"But even if I had, the tip was for serving drinks. If I was really going to sell sex on top of serving drinks, that would've been a separate service and deserves its own tip. Either way, you stiffed me."

Shade's smirk grew.

"Think I'm the one who got stiff and left hanging, if you want to get technical."

I smiled. I couldn't help it, even though I hadn't changed my mind. Shade was pretty. He might even be fun to play with, but he was still the kind of guy who'd trade a woman for a motorcycle.

Part of a motorcycle.

"I'm serious. I'm sorry that things were so weird and that Rebel put us into this situation, and I appreciate the ride home, but there won't ever be anything between us. I'm done with men. From now on it's just me and my vibrator."

Shade's gaze intensified. "What kind of vibrator you got?"

"I'm going inside now," I said, pushing against his chest. He ignored the gesture, leaning in to give me a soft, sweet kiss that left me aching. Then he let go, and I stepped away from the bike before I did something really stupid.

"We're not done," he reminded me. "But I get that you need to take care of your nieces. Oh, and I brought you a present."

He reached into a pocket inside his vest and pulled out a black rectangle.

"A phone?"

"You said yours was broken," he said. "This one works, although it's just a disposable. My number's already programmed into it, along with the landline at the clubhouse. You can also talk to Bone if you need to get hold of me. I'll see you later, probably tonight. Now get your ass inside and cook those girls something besides candy bars."

"Can I help make the macaroni and cheese?" Callie asked. She loved working with me in the kitchen, although I also got the sense she was stalling because she didn't want me leaving for my shift at the Pit. The girls loved it when I stayed home at night. A twinge of guilt twisted through me at the thought of how many evenings I'd wasted with Rebel.

"Let me cook the noodles first," I told her. "Then you can stir in the cheese packet."

Callie pouted, but she stepped to the side, giving me room to work. Hannah was back among the living, although she still looked like shit. She'd been getting these headaches her whole life, but I knew damned well that stress made them worse, and she'd had more than her fair share of that lately.

Worrying about me and my disappearing act last night probably hadn't helped.

At least the girls had been okay. I was still a little freaked out about what'd happened, especially Shade's "touched what was mine" comment about Rebel. The more I thought about it, the less comfortable I felt about the situation. Hopefully I wouldn't see the big Reaper tonight—I wanted to process and figure out my next step.

I should also get my ass in gear and get ready for work.

I'd need extra time to walk down because I'd left my bicycle there the night before. I'd also have to apologize to Bone for leaving him high and dry at work. Hopefully he wouldn't fire me before I found something else, which could take a while. Violetta wasn't exactly crawling with job opportunities. In the long run, I wanted to avoid bikers, but in the short term we needed the money.

I dumped the macaroni in the strainer, tossed it to get the water out and then poured it back in the pan. Callie dragged over a chair and climbed up to stir as I added the milk, the cheese packet and a glob of butter. Macaroni and cheese might not be the healthiest, but it tasted good and the kids loved it.

Hell, I loved it too.

Dishing up five bowls, I had Callie carry them to the table while I cut up a couple of apples for us to share. Then I joined Hannah and the girls at the table.

"It's gonna take a lot of makeup to cover that," Hannah said, nodding toward my face. I'd told her everything that'd happened already—we never kept secrets from each other.

"I know," I told her. "But it's not like I can stop working until it heals up. The bills won't pay themselves."

Hannah sighed. "They aren't your bills. You don't have to do this, you know. I hate feeling like I'm dragging you down with me."

I set down my spoon to look at my sister and her children. The twins were babbling at each other in the special little language that only they could understand, and Callie was very carefully sliding individual macaronis onto each of her fork tines.

Sometimes I loved them so much it hurt.

"We're a family. You and me, Hannah. We have to stick together because at the end of the day, we're the only ones we can count on."

They were Mom's words, repeated to us a thousand times during our childhood. Hannah smiled at me, then reached across the table to catch my hand, giving it a squeeze. It was true. She'd always been there for me. I'd stay here with her and the girls as long as they needed me.

We'd finished eating and I was dabbing my thickest concealer on my bruised face when I heard the sound of a motorcycle coming down the street. Make that motorcycles. They sounded like they were getting closer, too. *You're just being paranoid,* I told myself. *Finish getting ready for work.*

Then Hannah said, "Oh, shit" loudly from the living room. My hand stilled because Hannah didn't cuss in front of the kids. Ever. Outside the roar grew, coming to a stop in front of our house. I left the bathroom to join her at the window.

"What's wrong?" I asked, even though I had a pretty good idea. Sure enough, there were at least six bikers in the graveled street, all wearing the same matching colors. Reapers. Shade and his brothers were back.

Hannah and I shared a look.

"Girls, go play in your bedroom," she said quickly.

"Why?" Callie asked, holding a Barbie in one hand and a brush in the other. The twins stilled in the corner, where they'd been building with blocks.

Get them out of here! I mouthed at my sister. Hannah walked over to the freezer and pulled out a container of vanilla ice cream. Grabbing three spoons, she handed them to the children, then held the carton out to Callie.

"You can eat as much as you like so long as you stay in your bedroom," she said firmly. The little girl snatched the container out of her hand and disappeared before her mother could change her mind, the twins right behind her. Hannah turned back to me, all business. "Should I call the cops?"

"No," I said quickly. "I don't know why they're here, but I don't think we need to be afraid of them."

Probably.

"What do you want me to do?" Hannah asked.

"I'll go out and talk to them," I said, running a hand through my hair nervously. "You wait inside and make sure the girls stay out of it. And remember—the Reapers aren't the ones who threw me into the truck. They might be scary but they didn't actually do anything to hurt me."

"If I ever see Rebel again, I'm shooting him. For the record."

I snorted. "If Rebel's smart, he's headed for the hills. And knowing your luck, you'd shoot yourself in the foot if you had a gun."

"That's why I don't have one," Hannah admitted, peeking through the window again. "He's off his bike and headed for the door. Go see what he wants. I'll watch from in here and call the cops if they pull anything. Sound like a good plan?"

"Not really. You know I hate cops."

"Okay, then. I'll call your fairy godmother and ask her to rescue you."

I rolled my eyes, flipping her off as I stepped out the door.

Chapter Eight

I stepped out onto the old wooden porch, shutting the door behind me. Shade was almost across the lawn, although his fellow bikers were staying put. I guessed that was one small mercy.

"Why are you here?" I asked bluntly.

"Figured you'd need a ride to work," he replied. "Seeing as you had to leave your car at the bar last night."

"I don't actually have a car," I admitted. "I usually ride my bike to work."

Shade raised a brow. "You ride? I only ever saw you with Rebel. Don't tell me you gave up—"

"No!" I said, rolling my eyes. "Not a motorcycle. A *bicycle*. You know, the kind with pedals? That's how I get to work."

Shade's face turned serious. "You ride a bicycle home at two in the morning from the Pit?"

"Only on the busiest weekends," I said, shrugging. "We're usually closed by ten or eleven during the week. And what do you think's going to happen in Violetta anyway? Worst case, I get attacked by a deer."

He opened his mouth for a second, then closed it again, staring at me like I was some kind of exotic beast in a zoo. I frowned.

"I had a car," I told him. "But it was a piece of shit and I needed cash to move here, so I sold it. I'll get a new one at some point. Right now I'm focused on helping my sister, and it's only a couple miles to the Pit. No big deal."

"This isn't some city with bus lines and taxis," he said. "You can't just not have a car."

"And yet I don't," I said lightly. "So far, the car fairies haven't delivered one. Maybe they will tomorrow, but for today I'll go ahead and ride my bike."

Shade gave a low growl, which I decided to ignore.

"You told me your sister has kids—what does she do when they need to see the doctor?"

I looked away because it was a problem I'd been more than a little worried about. We needed to get the van up and running again, and soon. But we also needed to pay the power bill and buy food.

"There's always the ambulance," I said, smiling weakly. Shade shook his head slowly. "Her ex's parents have a car. I suppose we could borrow that if we really needed to."

"You gotta get this worked out, babe," he told me, his voice serious. "Violetta's a great little town, but there's not enough here for you to live without a vehicle."

No shit.

"Gee, thanks for pointing that out," I snapped, feeling defensive. "I guess I didn't understand until now that we were in a tough situation."

"Mandy, I'm sorry. I wasn't trying to—"

"No," I said, holding up a hand. "You don't get to come in here and judge us. Hannah's doing everything she can to give her kids a good life. She stayed in Violetta because her ex is a bastard but his parents aren't. They own the trailer and they let us live here for free, which is huge. Not only that, they're the girls' grandparents and they adore them. We move away from here, we move away from the only family they've got, and as someone who doesn't have much family myself, I know what a big deal that is. We'll get the car fixed and we'll get things figured out, but the last thing I want is some man in here trying to tell me what to do. Men cause problems—they don't solve them."

I took a deep breath, crossing my arms defiantly, waiting for him to argue.

"Okay," Shade said, nodding slowly.

"All right," I replied, feeling off balance. "I'm going back inside to get ready for work."

"Great, you can introduce me to your sister."

"What part of 'go away' are you not getting?" I asked, genuinely confused. "Have I done anything to encourage you? I don't want a man. I've had men and they cause nothing but trouble. The last one I had tried to trade me for a motorcycle, remember? The one before that got me—never mind. Let's just say he made Rebel look good."

"Glad to know the bar is set low," he said. "Makes it easier for me. You got a ride to work tonight?"

"No."

"So you're going to walk."

"Yes."

"Wouldn't it be less work to catch a ride, seeing as I'm right here and it's because of me that you don't have your bicycle? Not that I'm accepting blame—that's on Rebel—but it's not your fault you got caught up in any of this. Your situation is tough—you admit that. Why turn down someone offering you help just because he happens to have a dick?"

I opened my mouth to argue, then closed it because what he'd said made sense. Not only that, a ride would be nice.

"You promise you don't have any ulterior motives here?" I asked, and Shade laughed, shaking his head.

"Baby, you know damned well I have ulterior motives. I want to fuck you—think I've been clear on that point. But the fact is, you need a ride, I'm right here and either way the evening's gonna end the same. You'll spend the night serving drinks, I'll order a few, at some point I'll probably drag you into the back room and make out with you for a while, and then I'll leave you the tip you should've gotten last night."

My face flushed. What he said should've pissed me off, but I kept thinking about how it'd felt to wake up wrapped in his arms. *Guys are bad,* I reminded myself. *Didn't you learn anything from Rebel? McBride women can't afford to let men into their lives, not even for fun.*

Still, the bar was nearly three miles away and I'd be on my feet all night... Shade wrapped his hands around my waist, pulling my hips toward his. A thin tendril of traitorous desire twisted through me, spiraling up my spine and warming my stomach.

"Ask yourself this, Mandy. Last night I could've done anything I wanted to you. I'm the fucking president of the Reapers and we were on my territory. By the rules of the club I had every right to take you, and what did I do? I slept next to you like a fucking monk. You really think I'm gonna pull over on the side of the road and rip all your clothes off between here and the Pit? I'm not Rebel. I don't fuck around and I don't play games."

The words were blunt, matter of fact and they also happened to be true. Last night had been the recipe for rape, but it hadn't happened. *Yeah, but he still accepted you in trade for a bike,* Wonder Woman prodded.

Only part *of a bike, and he thought I was okay with it,* I reminded her.

"A ride to work would be nice," I said slowly. Shade's eyes flared with triumph, and his hands tightened on my hips. Then one slid up my back to my head, cradling it as his mouth slanted down over mine. His tongue slipped between my lips, invading so fast my head spun. It was a surprise attack—that was my only excuse for giving in so easily. I felt his other hand catch my ass, squeezing and pulling it into his body in a way that left no doubt that he was happy to see me.

Felt good. Way too good.

The blip of a police siren filled the air and we froze. Then Shade lifted his head, releasing me from his tight embrace while still keeping one arm firmly around my shoulders. Across the road, a county sheriff's car had pulled to a stop. The door opened to reveal a tall, lean man in a deputy's uniform who took in the scene, eyes flickering to my face.

I felt myself tense, the same way I did every time I saw a cop, and my heart sped up.

"You must be Mandy McBride," he said, surprising me.

"Um, yeah. I'm Mandy," I answered, wondering how he knew my name. Shade's arm tightened around my shoulder and the deputy's eyes narrowed.

"I'm Heath Andrews. I know your sister, Hannah. You look a lot like her. She works for my folks at the grocery store." His eyes flickered toward Shade. "Don't usually see the Reapers down here on the flat. Thought I'd stop by and make sure everything's okay."

Shit. Hannah must've called him. Probably panicked when Shade started kissing me...except there hadn't been enough time for that, had there?

Shade's club brothers had gone from being relaxed to something else. Alert. Focused. There was a tension in the air, and I knew in that instant that whatever rumors I might've heard about the local law enforcement being in bed with the Reapers, Heath Andrews wasn't part of it.

Interesting.

One of the bikers cracked his knuckles as Andrews took a step forward. The man was outnumbered, I realized. Outnumbered by a lot, but it didn't seem to faze him. He walked right up to me and Shade, eyes taking in the situation in a way that left me with no doubt that he saw everything.

"I'd like to speak with you and your sister inside, Ms. McBride," he said, the words casual but the tone firm. Shade's fingers tightened on my shoulder and I had a sudden, horrible realization.

Of course there hadn't been enough time for Hannah to call Andrews. Either this was a total coincidence, or he'd been planning to come here all along. *Holy shit, they really* did *kill Rebel and now he's come to question me!*

I felt my body start to tremble, a rush of fear and adrenaline filling me. I remembered the cops pulling up next to me in Missoula. I hadn't even been smart enough to realize I was in trouble. Nope, I'd been too busy Facebooking on my phone, for God's sake.

I'd waved hello to them.

Then I'd spent three nights in the county jail before a friend managed to bail me out, and I was *still* on probation. Sure, it was unsupervised probation—the prosecutor had thrown me a bone, seeing as I'd been clueless about the whole thing—but my record wasn't exactly clean.

Shit shit *shit!*

"I have to get ready for work," I told Andrews, the words coming out in a rush. "I have a shift down at the Pit and I can't be late. Can we talk another time?"

His eyes narrowed and a new tension filled the air.

"Ms. McBride, this won't take very long, but it's important that we talk. Would you mind stepping into the trailer?"

"You got a warrant?" Shade asked, his voice deceptively casual. Andrews shook his head slowly. Shade let me go, taking a step forward. "No warrant, no probable cause. Sounds to me like you got no reason to be here at all."

"Heath?"

My sister's voice was strained. I spun around to find her standing on the porch, halfway through the door.

"Ms. McBride," the deputy said, nodding his head to her. "I'd like to speak to you and your sister, if you don't mind."

"Of course—come right in," she said, flustered. I stepped away from Shade and moved toward my sister. I wasn't sure what was going on here, but I did know one thing. No way in hell I'd leave her alone with that cop if he'd come here because of me. This was my mess to clean up. Not hers.

Andrews started toward the steps, somehow never quite turning his back on the bikers. He didn't seem afraid or uncomfortable in the slightest, despite the fact that he was totally outnumbered.

"Would you be willing to join us?" he asked me again, polite but pointed.

"I'll come with you," Shade said.

"I need to speak with Ms. McBride alone," Andrews replied, and while his tone remained even, there was something in his voice that made it clear this wasn't a negotiation. Shade stiffened. We were about to have a badass showdown if I didn't do something.

"I'm happy to talk to you," I said, ducking out from under Shade's arm. He glanced down at me and I widened my eyes, willing him to go along with it. He didn't like the idea, but thankfully he decided not to force the issue in front of the deputy.

Heath waved me into the trailer, following me inside. Hannah closed the door behind us.

"Can I get you anything to drink?" she asked him, looking nervous. Not nervous in a I-did-something-wrong-and-the-cops-are-here kind of way. I knew all about that from my time with Trevor. No, this was cute-boy-is-talking-to-me-in-the-cafeteria-at-school nervous.

Oh. My. God.

Was my sister into the sheriff's deputy?

Andrews smiled. "Nothing to drink. I appreciate the offer, but I just wanted to be sure you ladies were all right. I don't usually see the Reapers around here. Figured I should check up on you."

"That's very nice," Hannah replied awkwardly, and any doubts I might've had disappeared. She *liked* him. How did I not know this already? I'd told her everything about Rebel, and the whole story about Shade, too. We always spilled—*always*. How had this gotten by me?

Except she knew how uncomfortable I felt around cops. She'd probably been scared to talk to me. Andrews turned to look in my direction.

"You've got some bruising on your face," he said quietly. "Do you feel safe with those men outside?"

"They're fine," I said quickly. "I got the bruises from falling..."

Gee, that sounded like a scene from a low budget PSA for battered women. Heath Andrews wasn't fooled for a minute.

"You can tell me what happened," he said. "I'll help protect you. The Reapers have a lot of influence in the area, but you don't have to put up—"

"No, it's really not that," I said, glancing between him and my sister. "Hannah, tell him. It wasn't the Reapers."

"It wasn't," she agreed. He caught her gaze and held it, assessing, then nodded.

"Then who was it?"

"I fell into a pickup truck," I said. "I mean, the side of it. I hit my head on the mirror. I was drinking."

Andrews studied me again. "You sure that's the story you want to go with?"

"It's the truth," I insisted, reminding myself that it was. I *had* been drinking last night and I'd definitely fallen into the mirror. I'd just left out the part about the fall happening after Rebel threw me. And to be fair, I'd punched him. "There's nothing here that needs investigating. I'm safe. Truly."

"She is," Hannah insisted. "I wouldn't lie to you, Heath."

Heath. Not Deputy Andrews. *Heath.* I shot my sister a look that promised we'd be talking later. She glanced away, blushing again.

"You sure you won't fall into any more trucks?" he asked. "You have choices, Mandy. I can protect you. There's a place where women can go."

He obviously didn't believe me… I needed to give him something more.

"Those bikers out there," I said, nodding toward the door. "I think they'll make sure there aren't any more trucks in my future. I mean, if for some reason I had trouble again. Which I won't."

"The Reapers are considered a gang by law enforcement," he told me, his voice serious. "Organized crime. Did you know that?"

"I understand, but they haven't done anything to me. Truly. This little…accident…had nothing to do with them. If anything, they helped me out of a tough situation. I don't have any reason to be afraid of them."

"All right," Andrews said. He looked to Hannah again. "I didn't see you downtown this morning."

Holy crap, they see each other often enough that he noticed she took a sick day! Hannah was a checker in Violetta's only grocery store, which meant she saw everyone in town, but she wasn't the *only* checker.

"You're going to be late for work if you don't head out soon," Hannah said, looking at me. I pulled out my new phone and realized she was right. Crap.

"Let me grab my stuff," I said. "Shade is giving me a ride."

Andrews didn't make any move to leave as I grabbed my bag, then ducked into the bathroom to check my hair and makeup. The bruise was still pretty obvious. Ugh. Hopefully it wouldn't show as much in the dim shadows of the bar. I took a second to text Hannah a quick "U OK with him? If not, send SOS" and then ran out the door, leaving the deputy still inside.

Shade stood waiting for me outside, body language all angry alpha.

Great. Just what I needed.

"Everything is fine," I told him. "He wanted to be sure you hadn't given me the bruise."

Shade snorted. "Fuckin' asshole. Just 'cause I ride a bike doesn't mean I beat up women."

"Actually, I think he was more concerned about Hannah," I replied. "Apparently they talk down at the grocery store or something. When he saw all of you here, he got worried."

Shade cocked a brow.

"Interesting. He single?"

"No idea," I said, shrugging.

"You tell him Rebel did it?" he asked, catching my hand and pulling me toward his bike. The other Reapers fell in beside us. I suddenly felt very short and small.

"I told him I fell into a truck, and that it wasn't going to happen again. He offered to help me get away if I needed it. I don't. That's about it. You don't need to worry—I didn't drag the Reapers and Rebel into anything."

"You think that's what I'm worried about?" Shade said, pulling up short. "Mandy, I made you a promise—anything that happens with Rebel won't come back on you. Not today, not ever. I don't need you lying to protect me. I'm a big boy."

"What makes you think I was trying to protect you?" I asked, trying to lighten the mood. "I'm the one who punched the asshole and smashed up his truck."

One of the other bikers—Dopey—snorted, and Shade turned to glare at him. I glanced back toward the trailer, wondering if Andrews was watching us through the window. How had things gotten so complicated so fast?

"Can you just give me a ride to work?" I asked Shade. "I'm running late and I need to talk to my boss."

"You got it, babe."

"I'm really sorry about last night," I told Bone. My boss sat behind his desk in the bar office looking grim and grumpy as usual. "I know you need to be able to count on me."

He leaned back in his chair, eyeing the bruise on my cheek.

"Rebel do that or Shade?" he asked bluntly.

"It wasn't Shade," I replied, refusing to answer fully. "And it won't happen again. The Reapers told him to disappear."

Bone gave a rare smile. "I take it Rebel's gone, then."

"I wouldn't know. We aren't talking."

Bone nodded thoughtfully, his smile vanishing as quickly as it'd appeared. "I suppose you think you're with Shade now?"

"Nope. I'd like to think I'm with myself," I told him, frowning. "Why does everyone around here assume that I have to be with a man?"

"Well, seeing as women don't ride with the Reapers, any girl who pulls up with them is with a man by definition. But Shade's not the type to have an old lady. I hope you realize that."

"I don't care what Shade is or isn't," I said, and it was almost true. "Last night was a mess. I don't know what you heard and I don't want to get into the details. I'm just glad I got through it and nobody got hurt."

"Aside from your face."

"I caused a hell of a lot more damage than he did," I snapped back. "Jesus Christ, you'd think I'm some wilting flower here or something. I fucked up, okay? I dated an asshole and he did what all assholes do eventually and fucked me over. As for the Reapers…I don't know what to think of them but I'm not looking to get involved there, either. All I want to do is take care of my sister and do my job. Is that really so much to ask?"

The words came out of me in a rush. Bone cocked a brow and then I realized what I'd just done. Bitched out my boss. Sure, I'd been thinking about trying to find a new job, but given the fact that I lived in a town of less than a thousand people and didn't have a car, available jobs weren't exactly jumping out at me.

"Sorry," I said, although the word didn't sound very sincere—probably because it wasn't. I wasn't sorry. I was *pissed.*

Bone shook his head.

"Christ, and to think I was worried about you," he said, leaning back in his chair. "But you keep that up and you'll be fine. Is Shade done with you?"

"Not my problem. I'm done with him."

Bone laughed, the sound more of a snort than anything. "Great attitude—too bad it doesn't work that way. You're done with him when he's done with you, not the other way around."

"I don't accept that."

"Well, this should be entertaining to watch," he said. "I realize you're all full of female empowerment and have things under control, but if I could offer a word of advice?"

"Sure," I said, trying to decide if he was making fun of me.

"Don't fall for him no matter what he says. These guys get hot for some girl and they go crazy. Treat her like a queen, convince her they can't live without her. You'll fall in love. Then he'll see someone else with a cute butt and it'll all be over."

"You do realize you're describing yourself, right?" I asked. Bone cracked another smile.

"Yup. That's why you should listen to me. Have fun with Shade if you want, but don't take him seriously. He's a short-term guy."

I sighed. "Bone, I don't think I've ever told you this, but I love strawberries."

"Most people do."

"Yeah, but most people aren't allergic to them. Damned things give me hives like you wouldn't believe. Sometimes I convince myself that I can handle just one. That if I only have a tiny taste, I'll be okay… Sure enough, half an hour later I'm puffed up like a balloon and red as a baboon's ass."

Bone studied me thoughtfully.

"And?"

"For me, men are like strawberries," I told him earnestly. "I've come to realize this. It doesn't matter how good they smell, if I get too close they'll poison me. That's why I'm giving them up—for my health. From now on, consider me your resident nun."

My boss smiled. "I don't usually see nuns wearing shorts that tiny."

I rolled my eyes. "Okay, so I'm a slutty nun who needs the tips. God understands. You gotta dress for success in this world."

"Yeah, this is gonna be entertaining as hell," he said. "Just don't come crying to me when he dumps you."

Chapter Nine

"You're going to have to talk to him sooner or later," Sara said, smirking at me. I glanced toward the back of the bar where the Reapers had taken up residence. So far I'd refused to have anything to do with them, insisting that Sara take care of their table.

Except Shade kept sending Sara back to me.

I'd assumed that if I just held out long enough, he would give up or they'd leave, but the man was stubborn.

"Sara's right," Bone said, laying down the law. "You need to get your ass over there."

"But I'm allergic to him—remember our talk?"

"Are you allergic to earning money?" Bone countered. "Because that's sort of my thing here. Earning money. I got seven guys back there who aren't drinking because my waitress won't serve them. Call me crazy, but I think you should do something about it before I get pissy."

I swore quietly.

"Bone's right for once," Sara agreed.

"So glad you approve," Bone said. "I been worryin' all night my waitresses won't agree with how I want to run my bar."

"Someone's grumpy," she replied, giving me a wink. "What's wrong, Bone—you get left high and dry last night?"

"Someday I'm gonna fire you for talking like that."

"Maybe some day, but not today." Laughing, she started toward the front of the bar, where a couple of fresh patrons had just found themselves a table. Bone's eyes followed her across the room. If I hadn't been so frustrated with the Shade situation, I might've called him on it.

Unfortunately, the Reapers were still waiting for their drinks and I couldn't risk losing my job. Sucking it up, I headed for their table, offering my brightest, fakest, most generic waitress smile.

"What can I get you gentlemen to drink?" I asked.

"'Bout fuckin' time," Dopey rumbled. "Been stuck waiting here for an hour."

"I'm so sorry—I thought you'd been helped," I said, ignoring Shade pointedly. "In fact, I could've sworn I saw Sara back here several times. Guess I need glasses. Now can I take your order, please?"

"Four pitchers," Shade said. "The usual. And some shots."

I hated how he just assumed that I'd know what he drank, except I actually did, and pretending I didn't would mean talking to him longer. Heading back toward the bar, I watched as the door opened and another group came in. More bikers. Bikers I recognized—Rebel's club.

Awesome.

I'd hung out with these people. Laughed with them. Eaten their food. Now I was the ex-girlfriend to one of their own—one whose truck I'd destroyed. One who might've gotten secretly murdered by the Reapers. Probably not, but… Oh, and then there was the bruising. Nothing awkward here, nothing at all.

Denial, I thought. *Denial will save me. Everything is good and at the end of the night, Bone will give all three waitresses shiny baby bonus unicorns because we're so Goddamned friendly and efficient.*

I really needed to get a new job.

"I'll be right with you!" I shouted out, heading back to the bar to put in Shade's order. At least Bone was smart enough not to gloat over the fact that I'd given in and served the Reapers.

I'd have hit him over the head with my tray.

Fortunately, things got busier after that, and while I was still keeping an eye on the Reapers, the bar was hopping for a Thursday night, which meant I didn't have much time to worry. By ten, it was clear this wouldn't be one of those evenings that we closed down early, even if it was a weeknight.

This was a good thing, too, because I liked money.

It also meant I was too busy running my ass off to think about the Reapers beyond making sure their drinks stayed full. Sara managed Rebel's club, who stuck to the front of the bar. Combined with my new philosophy of denial, this worked pretty well right up until I ran into his president's old lady in the bathroom.

We'd met before, of course. Her name was Amelia. She was at least twenty years older than me and she had a nice smile.

Except she wasn't smiling at me in the mirror.

Nope.

She was watching me patch up the pancake makeup I'd used to hide the bruising. I nodded, then washed my hands, desperate to get away before she had the chance to say something along the lines of *We all hate you now because you fed Rebel to the Reapers.*

Not that I had, but I couldn't exactly expect his friends to take my side in this whole thing.

"You're Mandy, right?" she asked. I nodded, noting she looked harder than I remembered. Hard in that skinny, wiry way that led me to believe she could kick my ass in a fight. "I heard about what happened."

"Um, yeah," I said, grabbing a paper towel. "Look, it wasn't—"

"Rebel's a moron and none of us are going to miss him," she said bluntly, catching me totally off guard. "The guys wouldn't say that, of course. I shouldn't even be talking to you about it, but this is awkward for everyone. What he did was a mark against our club and he's out bad. I'm sorry you got caught up in it."

I blinked, because whatever I'd expected her to say, this wasn't it. My mouth opened because I wanted to pepper her with questions. There were layers here. Layers that didn't quite make sense to me…but did I really want to know the answers?

I thought about Heath Andrews again and what it would feel like to get interrogated by him.

"Thanks," I said instead. Then I left the bathroom and went back to work.

"Time for a break," Bone told me an hour later as I passed him a tray of empties. It was just after eleven-thirty and he'd already sent Sara back for a rest.

"I'll be in the office," I replied, enjoying the thought of putting up my feet for a few. God only knew how late we'd stay open—hours at the Pit more or less followed the customers, and we could be here until two at this rate. Sara came up next to me.

"Anything I need to know?" she asked.

"The guys at table four are pretty fucked up," I told her. "We may need to cut them off soon."

Sara sighed, because cutting off customers was never fun.

"I'll do it," Bone said. "They're part of the riding club, which means their brothers might cause trouble."

"Thanks," Sara said, flashing him a quick smile.

"That's so sweet of you, Bone, stepping in like that. You know, you're wasted as a manwhore," I told him. "You'd make some lucky girl a wonderful boyfriend."

Sara burst out laughing and Bone growled.

"Break. Now."

I blew him a kiss and started toward the back of the bar, pointedly ignoring the corner full of Reapers. I might have to serve them drinks, but my break time belonged to me alone. My purse was locked up in Bone's office and I planned to grab it so I could touch up my makeup again.

I was halfway down the hall when the back room door opened and Shade stepped out, blocking my path.

"Hey, babe," he said, giving me a slow smile that made my ovaries combust.

"I'm not interested in talking to you," I said firmly. He ignored the words, sliding his hand into my hair to grip me tight for a deep, hard kiss that seemed to block out all other kinds of reality. How was I in his arms again? Wonder Woman would be so disappointed. I was vaguely aware that he'd tugged me into the room, but only fully grasped the situation as he kicked the door shut behind us. Then he was lowering me down onto a table, kicking my legs apart with his and pushing forward until my core touched the hard length between his legs.

It felt amazing. Whole body tingling type stuff.

This was when I really should've kicked him in the crotch.

Instead, I found myself tugging his shirt free from his jeans, sliding my hands up along the hard muscles of his back. Shade's tongue shoved deep into my mouth. Bursts of want and desire and raw need filled my body with fire, until it felt like I'd burn up entirely unless the empty ache between my legs was filled. Christ, no wonder he'd called me a cock tease. Every time he came near I melted into a puddle of hormonal glee.

Shade pulled back, panting as he stared down at me. I read all the same things I was feeling in his eyes. Whatever this was between us, it wasn't one sided and I wasn't the only one blown away.

"You can't tell me this isn't happening," he said, the words torn harshly from his throat. I wanted to deny it but I couldn't.

"I've never felt anything like it in my life," I admitted. He growled, all savage satisfaction at my admission. Then his hand twisted hard in my hair, bringing his mouth back down over mine. But kisses—even kisses as good as these—weren't enough anymore. My fingers dragged down his back, scoring deep as I demanded more. I wanted his mouth on my breasts, his hands between my legs…his cock deep inside. This was crazy and stupid and against everything I'd planned, but it felt so good.

So incredibly good.

Shade groaned as my nails drew blood, rearing back to slide his hands up and under my shirt. Then he cupped my breasts through my bra, fingers teasing the nipples. The intensity of feeling was almost more than I could take. My back arched and I moaned, ready to beg, when the door opened.

"Oh, shit! I had no idea. I'm so sorry!" someone said. Sara. It was Sara. She'd walked in on us, just like anyone could walk in on us because I was halfway to fucking a man I barely knew in a bar on my break.

Holy.

Fucking.

Shit.

Reality crashed down around my ears as I pulled away, mortified. Shade growled, catching me by the waist and jerking me back into his body.

"No."

"Yes," he said, eyes narrowed. "You want this. I want this. There's no fucking reason on earth we should stop."

"No," I said again, daring him with my eyes. "You don't get to decide. I get to decide and I am not doing this at work where anyone can walk in on us."

Triumph flared in his expression, throwing me off guard. Then I realized what I'd said. *Crap.* "I meant we aren't doing this at all. I don't want a man in my life."

He shoved a hand down my pants, sliding past my panties to dip a finger into the hot crevice between my legs. I gasped as he rubbed my clit, my back arching as he slid deeper. Then his hand was out again. Holding my gaze steadily, he lifted his fingers to his mouth and slowly licked one.

"Tastes good," he whispered. "Tastes like you want me. I think you're lying, princess. You want it and you want it bad."

My entire body clenched because he was right. I wanted him real bad. So bad it hurt.

"Let me go," I said, the words causing me physical pain. "You're sexy. You know that. And maybe I do want it. But I can't afford any more mistakes. I have responsibilities and a life that you'll ruin if you touch it. I can't take the risk."

There was frustration written all over Shade's face, but he took a step back, the tiny muscle in his jaw clenching as he fought for control. I pushed myself upright, straightening my shirt as I tried to catch my breath.

"I need to get back to work," I gasped. "This is all a game for you—it's about getting laid—but it's my *life*. I have to take care of my family and you're getting in the way of me doing that."

"Bone won't fire you for taking a longer break. Not if you're with me. I'm the fucking president of the Reapers MC—nobody stands in my way."

"You don't get it," I said, closing my eyes. I couldn't look at him. Not like this. He was too sexy and I'd forget why I was fighting him. "It's not about what I can get away with. It's about who I am. I'm a good worker and I don't slack off. And maybe I was stupid enough to let myself get distracted by Rebel, but that doesn't mean this is my new reality. I'm getting my life on track again. Right now, I've got a job and I'm going to do it the best I can. This is nothing more than a game to you, anyway, so go find someone else to play it with."

We stared at each other for long seconds. Then Shade turned and stalked out of the room. I flopped back down on the table, lifting my legs to lie on my side in a fetal position.

Fucking hell but I needed a new job.

Fast.

It took me nearly ten minutes to pull myself together and get back to work. By that time the Reapers were gone.

Thank you, sweet baby Jesus.

"You okay?" Sara asked as I grabbed my tray.

"Yeah, I'm fine," I told her, although I felt like I'd gotten hit by a truck. "Shade and I…"

"I know," she said. "These guys… You can't control them. They're like a force of nature."

"I never asked for this," I insisted. "I didn't mean to catch his eye and now I don't know how to get rid of him."

"Just keep going," she said, watching Bone with pain-filled eyes. "He'll get bored. They always do. All of the fucking men in this place do."

I glanced toward Bone, who was leaning forward against the bar, flirting with yet another girl. One I hadn't seen before.

"Why do you stay?" I asked her. Sara gave me a startled look.

"What do you mean?"

"It's got to hurt, watching him like that."

"Where am I supposed to go?" she admitted. "There's no other jobs in this fucking town. Am I supposed to work for Handsy Randy, the friendly town drug dealer down at the gas station? I know you're related, so no offense."

"None taken," I said with a sigh. "But you could leave. It's not like you're married or have kids or anything tying you down."

"My grandma," she replied quietly. "She raised me. Now I'm the only one she has left. Maybe someday when she's gone… But for now, this is where I stay. This is my place. And maybe I do have a thing for Bone, but I've been there, done that."

"Really?" I said, startled. "You've slept with Bone?"

"Hon, *everyone* has slept with Bone," she replied, shrugging. "That's the problem. And that's why you can't let yourself get hung up on Shade. If it was me, I'd just go for it. Have fun while you can and then walk away. It's easier than fighting."

I stared at her, stunned. Sara was always full of energy, always smiling, always ready for the next challenge. Or so I thought. In that instant, though…she looked tired. Tired and sad.

That's why you can't give in. Because he'll leave you like that. Sad and alone.

"You girls gonna clear those tables and serve more drinks or what?" Bone shouted. I caught Sara's hand, sharing a quick squeeze, then grabbed my tray to go clear the Reapers' empties and wipe down their tables. That's when I found the money, a stack of hundred dollar bills, just sitting out on the table like it was a perfectly normal and appropriate thing.

I grabbed the cash, counting it carefully, my heart starting to clench. Five hundred dollars.

Five.

Hundred.

Dollars.

The Reapers had been drinking all night, but this wasn't some city bar. Drinks were cheap here at the Pit. Even factoring in all they'd ordered, there was no way this could be right. I stuffed the money in my apron pocket and then scurried over to Bone, feeling almost sick to my stomach. He was still chatting up his girl but I didn't care—we needed to figure this out, and fast.

"How much was their tab?" I hissed at him. Bone raised a brow.

"Whose?"

"The Reapers!" I snapped, as if there could be any other answer.

"About two hundred," he said. "But they already paid."

I pulled the wad of cash out of my pocket.

"Shade left this on the table," I told him. "What do I do with it?"

Bone shrugged. "Put it in your pocket. He left it for you."

"I can't keep a tip this big," I insisted.

"Well, I suppose you could try giving it back," Bone said. "But I got a feeling he wouldn't take it. This is his game, Mandy. If you're smart, you'll make the most of it while you can."

"I don't want to play," I insisted. "I don't like this game. I don't understand the rules."

"Then you better leave town," Bone replied, his voice serious. "Otherwise you got to play it out to the end. There's no in between when it comes to the Reapers. You want to fight with him about it, be my guest, but I think you should take the fucking money. God knows you need it, so use it."

He turned back to his girl, giving her a slow smile that left me with no doubt how his night would end. I glanced over to find Sara watching us. She gave me a shrug, and I realized Bone was right.

I needed the money, just like everyone else in this shithole of a town.

Goddamn but Violetta sucked, and so did the Reapers MC.

By the time I finished my shift, I was exhausted. Not just the normal tired that came from being on my feet all evening, but from taking care of the girls and the fact that I'd been up the night before dealing with Rebel and Shade.

It was just too much stress in too short of a time.

Not only that, I felt the weight of the money sitting in my apron pocket the entire time. Men didn't just give waitresses tips like that. It was too much—way too much. And the fact that it matched the amount he'd offered Rebel for sleeping with me...well, let's just say the implication wasn't comforting.

Back home, I tossed and turned on the couch for several hours, unable to sleep. By four in the morning I gave up, stepping out onto the porch to look up at the night sky. Summer was short in Idaho, which meant there weren't many nights a girl could sit outside and look at the stars without freezing her ass off, but this was one of them. Everything was still and peaceful. For a few minutes, I pretended I was living in a world where bad things didn't happen to innocent people.

Except they did.

I'd gone to jail because my ex-husband had robbed a liquor store while I sat waiting in the car outside like a moron. My sister was barely surviving on food stamps and Medicaid because her ex was a loser who couldn't be bothered to support his kids. And I had five hundred dollars in my pocket that I couldn't explain—five hundred dollars given to me by a man who'd almost certainly done worse things than my ex ever dreamed of doing.

Money that might implicate me in some crime I couldn't even imagine. He hadn't left me a tip—he'd left me a ticking time bomb.

I pulled out the cheap phone Shade had given me and powered it on, searching for his contact information. Then I sent him a text.

Me: Thanks for the tip but I cant keep it. I'll put it in an envelope and leave it with Bone. You can pick it up the next time ur at the bar. I cant get involved with a man like you so take it back

I hesitated for an instant before hitting *send*, then stuffed the phone back in my pocket, resolved. Then I lay back down on the porch and studied the stars. They really were gorgeous. Bright and beautiful and glorious and free. I'd only spent three nights in jail, but it'd felt like three years. I'd missed the stars most of all, which had surprised me. I never considered myself much of a nature girl. I guess you don't realize how much something matters to you until you lose it.

The phone buzzed in my pocket.

Shade: Keep the money.

Me: No I cant. You seem to think I'm not serious when I say I don't want a man but I am. I want to work and earn my money and take care of my sister. You don't know me and you don't know all the reasons I feel this way but they're real and that should be enough.

Shade: Then tell me.

Yeah, right. Like I'd be sharing my past with him. No fucking way I'd give him more leverage over me. I turned off the phone and looked back up at the stars, wondering if I'd ever truly be free.

Probably not.

Pisser.

Chapter Ten

Friday morning

"Can we take some ice cream with us?" asked Callie.

"No way," I told her, rolling my eyes. "Ice cream will melt at the park."

"Not if we bring a bag of ice cubes with it," she insisted, looking determined. "Mommy loves ice cream."

"I think the sandwiches will be enough," I told her. "And Mommy is trying to eat healthy, remember?"

Callie sighed heavily, making it clear that I was the meanest auntie in the history of time. Maybe she was right. This suited me just fine, seeing as I was also the brokest and most confused auntie, too. I'd defiantly put the $500 in an envelope and left it with Bone, determined to ignore Shade the next time he came to the bar.

Except there hadn't been a next time.

Here we were, two days later, and I hadn't seen or heard from the sexy Reaper, which was exactly what I'd wanted, except it was also one hell of a blow to the ego.

There's something broken in your brain, idiot. Obviously, he's a lot less hung up on you than you thought. This is a good thing. It's what you wanted. Now get over yourself.

Grabbing the plastic grocery bag carrying our lunch, I gathered up the girls and herded them out the door. At three years old, the twins were big enough to walk, but it made things a lot easier if we took the stroller, so that's what we did. Violetta's one small park was just over a mile away, located right in the center of town across from the grocery store. It was an interesting place—possibly one of the last parks in America with a merry-go-round (made of rusty metal, naturally) and wooden slides.

The girls and I had made a habit of meeting Hannah there for lunch when the weather was nice. Her break ran from twelve-thirty to one, which gave her just enough time to wolf down a sandwich and then push the girls on the swings for a while. By the time we made it back to the house, they'd be tired and ready for their naps, which was a win for everyone.

Hannah was already there when we arrived.

"Thanks, baby doll," she told Callie, who handed her a peanut butter and jelly that'd somehow gotten smushed along the way, despite my best efforts.

"I made it with extra love," Callie insisted. "And some Rice Krispies, so it's crunchy. Can I go play now?"

"Sure," Hannah said, and the little girl took off, followed by her sisters. I leaned back on my hands, watching as they attacked the monkey bars. "So, still no word from the sexy biker guy?"

"Nope," I replied, refusing to look at her.

"And the money is still just sitting there at the bar?"

"Yup."

"I realize that you're being all noble and principled," she said slowly. "But five hundred bucks would probably be enough to get the van up and running. We're going to need it once the weather turns."

"It's going to take more than that to get that thing running again," I muttered. "They said at least a thousand, with a miracle thrown in for good measure."

Hannah reached down, twisting her finger in the grass thoughtfully. "I talked to Heath about it. His family has a farm shop and he's a pretty decent mechanic. He thinks he could help us out if I had the money for parts."

I turned to stare at her.

"Heath?" I asked, raising a brow. "I thought you and the good deputy were just friendly acquaintances."

She shrugged, refusing to meet my eyes.

"You *insisted,*" I continued. "You swore to me that there was nothing going on between you guys. It was a pinkie swear."

"I didn't want to freak you out," she admitted, blushing. "I know you aren't a big fan of cops."

"No, I'm not a big fan of jail," I said. "And if you remember correctly, that's exactly where I'm headed if someone decides I violated my probation. The last thing I need is some sheriff's deputy watching everything I do. If we get the van running, I'll run a light or something, and then he'll arrest me and I'll go to prison and be someone's bitch. Someone named Rhonda or Kaleee with three E's. I can see it now."

"The probation's just a formality and you know it," she said, rolling her eyes. "You aren't even being supervised. They gave you the minimum because you were as much a victim as anyone. They didn't even have a problem with you moving here."

"You're not the one who went to jail."

"You were there for three days, and the only reason it was that long was because you didn't have bail money. Get over yourself."

I glared at her.

"I can't believe you're falling for a cop."

"I can't believe you aren't taking that five hundred bucks and fixing the van," she snapped. I looked away, feeling pissy because she was probably right. We really did need to fix the Kia and Shade obviously wasn't in a hurry to get his money back. He also wasn't in a hurry to see me.

So much for "this isn't over yet" and all that smoldering, sexy intensity of his.

This is about your ego. Snap out of it.

Stupid men.

As if summoned by my thoughts, a sheriff's car pulled into the parking lot. I could all but smell Hannah's excitement.

"You're a slut," I told her glumly.

"Yeah, well, you're just jealous," she replied, sounding perky. "And he's a nice guy. Exactly the kind of guy we never date."

"That's why we shouldn't be dating at all," I reminded her. "Mom was shit at it, I'm shit at it and so are you. You just wait and see—he's going to strap you to the train tracks while a train is coming, then stroke his mustache and cackle. It's our destiny as McBride women."

"He doesn't have a mustache."

A clump of grass hit me in the side of the head. I turned on her, grabbing my own clump to throw as she screamed. Callie and the little girls came running, jumping on their mom in excitement. She managed to send me a death glare and I knew I'd pay for making her look silly in front of her new boyfriend. Too fucking bad.

"Totally worth it," I mouthed at her, then I looked up at Heath Andrews and smiled.

"My sister's crazy," I told him. "You should run away while you still can."

The twins were sound asleep in the stroller by the time we got home, exhausted from playing with Callie, Hannah and Heath. My sister and her deputy looked so adorable together that I could've barfed. Even worse was the way he watched her—the man was crazy about Hannah.

Obviously, he was a secret serial killer.

Only possible explanation.

The sidewalk disappeared once I passed the railroad tracks, which made pushing the stroller a hell of a lot harder. Nothing quite like tiny plastic wheels on gravel for a smooth ride. That's probably why I didn't notice the old pickup truck parked next to the trailer until we were nearly on top of it.

"Daddy's here!" Callie shouted, her little voice full of joy. I felt sick to my stomach because I remembered those days from my own childhood. My father had been in and out of our lives until I was about six. Then he was out for good and I never saw him again. It took another few years before I realized he wasn't coming back, and even longer before I understood it wasn't my fault.

Now I was watching the same scenario playing out with my nieces and Randy, Hannah's loser of an ex.

A loser of an ex who was apparently waiting inside the trailer, despite the fact that he didn't have a key. I must've forgotten to lock it when we left for the park.

Hannah was gonna kill me.

Callie took off running and I pushed the stroller faster, wondering why the hell he'd finally decided to visit. He lived nearby but we never saw him, even though it would take less than ten minutes for him to swing by and see his own kids.

I'd love to say I'd been surprised by how things had turned out, but I really wasn't. Randy had never been a winner. The first time I'd met him, he'd gotten drunk and made a pass at me, but Hannah was pregnant and in love. I wasn't going to be the one to burst her happy little bubble.

Right after Callie was born, he'd been arrested for possession. He'd gotten less reliable after that and started cheating on Hannah with Vera Blount. Vera was ten years older than him and had gotten money in her divorce. Six months ago he'd taken off to buy a pack of smokes and never came back. Hannah had finally acknowledged reality and changed the locks when she learned they were living together.

Better late than never.

"You've been growing!" Randy was telling Callie, all smiles as I walked in with the twins. He glanced up at me and his expression was a lot less friendly. Fair enough—the feeling was mutual.

"What are you doing here?" I asked bluntly.

"Stopped by to see my girls," the bastard replied, his voice so sweet I wanted to vomit. "You know I've been missing you, don't you baby?"

Callie hugged him hard, although I noticed the twins didn't seem the slightest bit interested. Probably couldn't remember who he was.

"Callie, can you go into your room for a few?" I asked, forcing myself to stay polite. The little girl frowned, but she followed my instructions. The twins followed as usual, muttering in their own little language. I waited until they were out of earshot and then laid into him. "You aren't supposed to be here, Randy."

"Last I checked, I owned this trailer."

"No, your parents do," I corrected. "And they're as sick of your shit as the rest of us. Unless you're here with a child support check and your balls in a jar, you need to get the hell out."

"I have a right to see my children," he said, taking a step toward me. His stance was anything but friendly, and it suddenly occurred to me that maybe I shouldn't be picking fights when there weren't any witnesses.

Little late for that now.

"Hannah has a lease from your parents," I reminded him. "It's all official. You're trespassing, and if you don't leave I can call the sheriff and have you thrown out."

"The sheriff spending a lot of time here these days?" he asked, the question a snarl. "I hear things. Hannah's fucking a deputy, isn't she?"

"Hannah's working hard to support her children," I countered, his visit suddenly making sense. He didn't want Hannah, but he didn't want anyone else to have her either. Typical. "And what she does in her private life is none of your business. You need to leave. Now."

"Or what?"

"Try me and find out," I bluffed, because I had no idea what the hell I'd do. Bite him, maybe? *You'd probably catch something.* Randy locked eyes with me and I held my ground, praying desperately he'd back down. Finally, he shook his head slowly, laughing.

"You're fucking pathetic, Mandy," he said. "But I was leaving anyway. Tell Hannah not to bother changing the locks again. There's nothing she can do to keep me out of here. Those kids are mine, this house is mine, and she's mine, assuming I want her fat ass, which I don't. Make sure she knows it, too."

He started toward the door and I held my breath, praying he'd actually leave. When it shut behind him I ran over and tried to lock it, only to discover he'd broken the deadbolt. The metal had held, but the door frame itself was so weak and rotten that it'd crumbled like cardboard.

Fucking hell. At least I hadn't forgotten…

Pulling out my phone, I sent Hannah a quick text.

Me: We got a problem. Randy was here. I made him leave but I think he'll be coming back soon. He broke in

Hannah: Shit

Me: Pretty much. I fucking hate this town. For the record.

Hannah: We'll figure it out. Heath might be able to help

Me: Sure and I'll just give Shade a call too. Maybe Rebel. If we get enough men here that'll totally solve the problem.

Hannah: Don't be such a bitch

Me: Sorry

Hannah: Its ok. We WILL figure this out. Just hang in there. Love you

Me: Love you too. Gonna go check on the kids now. Be careful walking home.

Hannah: I think Heath is giving me a ride

Of course he was. I still didn't like the idea of the guy, but better him than Randy. Of course, best of all would be us figuring out a way to get through this on our own.

Yet another thing to add to Future Me's to do list. Poor thing was going to be crushed under the weight of it at this rate.

Chapter Eleven

It was almost a relief when I clocked in at the bar that night. I'd been dreading going in to work for two days because I didn't want to see Shade.

Randy's visit had offered me some perspective.

Shade I understood. He was a bad guy, definitely. A threat. But he was a threat to me and me alone—I didn't need to worry about him hurting my sister and her family.

I couldn't say the same about Randy.

Me and Hannah had talked more once she'd gotten home, trying to figure him out. We were both confused about why Randy had come to the house because he sure as shit didn't give a damn about her or the kids. Her theory was that he'd hidden some money there, which made as much sense as anything. I had a bad feeling, though. The same kind of feeling I'd gotten while I was waiting for Trevor in the liquor store parking lot, when the cop knocked on my car window.

The fact that she was all bright-eyed and bushy-tailed about Deputy Hottie didn't make me feel any better, either.

I'd seen his kind before.

Heath was a good guy, but he walked a straight line. He'd follow the law, and I knew all too well how easy it was to find yourself as an accessory to a crime, especially with a guy like Randy hanging around. It'd been one thing for me to get wrapped up in that, but if Hannah got arrested, what would happen to the kids? They'd probably haul me off with her, seeing as I lived there and was already on probation. That left Randy's parents to watch the girls, and they weren't exactly qualified.

Loving grandparents they might be, but they'd created him in the first place. Throw in the health problems and they were essentially useless. Sad but true.

Randy needed to go away. Preferably Heath, too, because the last thing we needed was a lawman sniffing around. I didn't care how cute he was.

Fortunately, tonight should be busy enough to distract me from worrying about it. Bone was expecting a decent crowd because he'd brought in a band, something we didn't see that often in Violetta. That meant both Sara and Suz were working with me.

This turned out to be a very a good thing because right after the second set, the Reapers showed up.

All of them.

Nearly thirty guys, plus their women, liquored up and ready to party. Now we'd be busting ass until the wee hours. Bone didn't believe in shutting down the bar when there was still money to be made, no matter what the law said. The liquor control board didn't exactly have a branch office in Violetta.

In a way, this was a blessing.

I hadn't seen Shade since the night he'd left me the giant tip, and now I could pretend I was too busy to talk to him, which was sort of the truth. It was embarrassing to admit, but I halfway expected him to play the same game that he had before and refuse service from anyone but me. Then Suz went over to take their order and he didn't even glance in my direction.

He didn't glance in my direction when the music started, either, or when a group of college girls who'd come slumming went over and started chatting him up.

Nope, Shade was having a grand old time.

Bastard.

You wanted him to leave you alone, I reminded myself. *You told him to find someone else to pester because you aren't interested in him. You even insisted that he take back his five hundred bucks and forget you ever existed, remember?*

Except the longer I watched him with those little bitches, the harder time I had remembering why I'd been so hell-bent on keeping him out of my bed. Things got even worse when Sara gave me a pat on the shoulder, along with one of those little sympathy smiles girls offer each other when a relationship falls apart.

"I need a break," I told Bone.

"We got a full house in here," he reminded me. "You sure it can't wait?"

I crossed my arms and glared at him.

"Okay, I guess you're due," he said, although I could tell it pissed him off. Tough shit. By law I was allowed a break every two hours, no matter how busy we were. The fact that we usually let those slide in exchange for more flexibility on slow nights didn't matter to me—I needed to get the hell away from Shade and his harem.

Tossing my apron down behind the bar, I headed out back for some fresh air. There was a small covered porch out there for the staff, along with a few battered chairs and a picnic table that'd seen better days. Slamming the door behind me, I boosted myself up onto the table and pulled out my phone.

That's when the door opened again and Shade stepped outside to join me.

"What the fuck do you want?" I demanded.

"What's the matter—you on the rag?" he asked, smiling even though he had to know that'd piss me off.

"You're such a fucking pig. Where the hell do you get off, coming out here and talking to me like that?"

"You're the one who bit my head off," he said, leaning back against the door and crossing his arms. He cocked his head at me, studying my figure. "So what's the answer?"

"To what?"

"Are you on the rag?"

My mouth dropped and I stared at him, stunned.

"What the hell is wrong with you?" I finally managed to ask.

"Nothing," he replied, giving me a slow grin. "Just trying to figure out how sloppy it's gonna be."

Oh, no way. *He didn't just go there*…except he had. He totally had.

"Get the hell out of my sight," I hissed. "Go fuck one of your college girls if you're horny."

"But I don't want to fuck one of them. I want to fuck you."

"Not happening."

"We'll see," he said, taking a step toward me. "Is that what crawled up your butt and died? Seeing all those girls in there? Or are you pissed that I didn't make you serve me? Mixed signals, baby. You should really work on that," he added with a grin.

"I don't give a shit what you do," I told him, which was a damned lie. *Asshole.*

"Yeah, I think you do," he said, stepping in to me. He put one hand on either side of my body and I leaned back to avoid contact. Shade pushed a knee between my legs, taking advantage as he gave a low laugh. "You can't stop thinking about me, can you?"

"I've been thinking about all the reasons I hate bikers," I said. "And I'm not for sale. Bone has your five hundred bucks—you can pick it up on the way out. Use it for one of your cheap whores."

Shade shook his head slowly. "I'm only interested in one girl tonight and I'm pretty sure she's not a whore. Hell, considering all you went through, I think you earned the money fair and square. Just don't expect any more after we fuck. You already made it clear you aren't for sale and I can respect that."

I raised a hand to slap him, but he caught it, deftly twisting it around behind my back, pushing me forward into his body. Then his mouth took mine, teeth nipping at my lips until I opened for him. His other hand grabbed my ass and then I completely forgot why I hated him so much.

Shade

Watching Mandy twitch her butt and flirt with every man in the whole fucking bar was pure torture. She'd worn a jean skirt so short it just barely skimmed the top of her thighs, practically begging me to jerk it up and bury my cock in that tight snatch of hers.

I remembered how it tasted.

Couldn't sleep at night without jerking off, that's how much I remembered it. Nearly killed me, but I'd given her space the last couple days. She was skittish and I knew I'd lose her if I didn't play the game right.

Tonight, though…tonight I'd had enough waiting.

I'd come to the Pit with every intention of claiming her and I'd be doing it, too. When I'd followed her out onto the back porch I'd planned to kiss her, maybe tease her a little. Get her off. Then I'd convince her to hop on my bike and I'd show her what a man like me had to offer.

The instant I tasted her, though, I forgot all about taking it slow. She had no fuckin' clue how sexy she was or that she could have any man she wanted. Somehow that made it even hotter when I finally shoved my tongue into her mouth.

Watching her settle for that limp-dicked fuckwad, Rebel, had nearly killed me.

It'd been bad enough when they'd still been together, but once I'd had a taste, I knew I wouldn't be able to walk away. Not until I'd had all of her. Repeatedly. With some women, once was enough. You got the itch, you scratched it and then you lost interest. Mandy was more. I had no fuckin' idea why and I didn't care, because that wasn't how I lived my life. I took what I wanted, enjoyed the hell out of it and then moved on.

I wasn't under any illusions about the situation.

I'd be leaving soon, swinging back through Portland for a few months in my role as club president, and she'd stay in Violetta. Girls wanted flowers and roses and forever. I wanted the road under my tires and something new on the horizon. Never understood why so many of my brothers were willing to settle down in one place.

I wasn't that guy.

Never had been. Never would be.

But Mandy…I was starting to realize I wanted more than a quick roll in the sack with her, even if it meant delaying for a while. The itch was bad and it'd take time to scratch it right. Time I fully intended to spend buried deep inside that tight little pussy of hers.

Time I'd only get if I stuck to my strategy, a fact I completely forgot as I grabbed her ass, jerking her tight into my body. Her skirt was up around her waist and the only things separating us were a few thin scraps of fabric. My tongue filled her mouth, thrusting deep like I would with my cock.

Goddamn that was good.

Fuckin' turn-on from hell, actually. So was the fact that I could do whatever I wanted with her out here. Nobody could stop me, not with my brothers watching my back. Might make me a bastard but that was the reality.

Reaching down, I slid my hand between us, finding her clit, rubbing and circling it as we kissed. My cock was so hard it hurt and my balls were drawn up, tight and ready to go. I still held one of her hands tight, but she pushed the other one between us, catching my fingers and shoving them into her panties.

Holy. Fucking. Hell.

I pulled away from her mouth, staring down as she worked her clit, using my fingers like she owned them. I let her other hand go. She reached around to fumble with the fly of my jeans, tugging at it, desperate for my cock. Catching the fabric, I ripped it loose, shoving down my pants as her fingers wrapped around the hard length of my dick.

I'd never been much of a believer, but in that moment I saw Heaven and it was glorious.

Mandy wasn't gentle, squeezing hard as she worked me, jerking her fingers up and down so fast that she'd make me come unless I stopped her. Hooking one finger in her panties, I jerked the soft fabric to the side, clearing a path before plunging my cock into her cunt, hard and deep.

She bit my shoulder, moaning as I stilled for long seconds, savoring the sensation. Then I pulled back slowly and slammed into her again. I wanted to stay there—frozen in time—but my cock had other ideas. My hips started moving until I was pounding hard.

Jesus Christ but that was good.

Too good, I suddenly realized. How the hell was I gonna pull out at the last minute? I hadn't rubbered up, but I sure as shit wasn't ready to be a daddy. Her muscles were slick, squeezing me so tight it should've been painful, but instead it was perfect.

Better than perfect.

It felt like coming home.

Reaching down, I started working her clit again, sensing what she needed by the way her body bucked and jerked against mine. Then her back arched and she screamed, clamping around me like she wanted to rip my dick off—a sacrifice I'd probably be willing to make under the circumstances. Mandy's orgasm rippled around me, her inner muscles squeezing again and again as she moaned my name. I thought my head might explode from the need raging through my body. At the last second I managed to pull out, shooting my spunk on her thighs instead of where it belonged, gasping like my world had just ended.

In a way it had.

I'd fucked a lot of girls, but never like this. Never dreamed it was even possible. Mandy might be stubborn and annoying and a pain in the ass about money, but holy fucking hell.

For the first time in my life, I couldn't imagine riding out for the next city without taking a woman with me.

You fucked up, man. This is gonna get complicated.

Chapter Twelve

Mandy

"Wow…" I said, slowly blinking my eyes.

Shade was still between my legs, his pants wide open and my skirt up around my waist. We'd just had the best sex of my life and my brain wasn't quite ready to start working again. Still, it felt like there was something really important I'd forgotten.

Condom, Wonder Woman pointed out acidly.

Oh my God, I was so stupid. That was the curse of the McBrides—men made us so fucking *stupid.*

"'Wow' is good," Shade murmured in my ear, giving me a soft kiss. "Holy fuckin' shit works better. What the hell just happened?"

"I don't know, but I kind of want to do it again," I admitted, mind racing. "Next time with a condom. I have some in my purse. Does that make me sound slutty? Never mind, I don't care. I totally want to do that again. A lot. But only if you don't have a disease. I can't believe we didn't use a condom."

Shade shook his head slowly. "Me either. I always suit up."

"Thank fuck for that," I said fervently, the filter between my brain and mouth completely overloaded. "That was really good sex. Like, the *best* sex. I remember that I'm supposed to be pissed at you but right now I can't remember why. Oh, and I'm disease free too. For the record. And I've got an implant, so there's that."

No fucking way I wanted to end up like my sister.

Shade reached down, tracing the edge of my face and then trailing his fingers down between my breasts. My push-up bra and tank top served them up on a platter, but we hadn't had time to go there yet.

Did I want to go there?

Yes. Yes, I did. He might be a pig and all sorts of wrong, but the damage was done. I was only human—not even Wonder Woman could hold out forever, not in the face of that kind of chemistry.

Shade's eyes darkened as he found my nipple. I shivered, wishing I'd brought my purse out with me. Then the music from the bar suddenly got louder, breaking the spell. *Must be the band starting their next set.*

Band.

Bar.

"I'm still at work!" I shoved Shade away as I sat up, grabbing the bottom of his T-shirt to wipe at my wet, sticky thighs. Oh my God, I really *was* a slut. A dirty bar slut. Even worse, I was a bar slut who had to go back to work with a biker's come all over my legs, because that's how I rolled. "This is a new low for me."

Shade snorted. "What're you so worried about? You're with me—your boss won't have a problem with it. Let's get the hell out of here and do it right. You know, in a bed with a little more privacy."

"Tempting," I told him, which was the truth. "But that'd be screwing over Suz and Sara, and I've got a feeling that in a month you won't even remember my name. Then I'll need one of them to cover a shift for me for something important, like taking care of my nieces, and they'll tell me to fuck off. Unless you plan to stick around and take care of my nieces?"

Shade stared at me, blinking. I realized it was probably the first time a woman had ever talked to him that way.

Good girl, whispered Wonder Woman.

"Don't get me wrong," I said, tugging my skirt into place. Ugh. I seriously needed to wash my hands. "Theoretically, it'd be great to do this again, and that part with the bed sounds nice. I just really need to get back to work right now before I get in trouble. That whole thing with Rebel was bad enough—I don't want to make the same mistake twice. You're just getting laid but this is my life. I can't afford to let you fuck it up."

With that, I hopped off the table and left him behind.

"Are you okay?" Sara asked, slapping her tray down on the bar pass-through. She'd watched me come back from my break with anxious eyes, but it'd taken half an hour before we managed to run into each other at the bar. "I saw Shade following you outside."

"Three more pitchers and a round of shots for table seven," I shouted at Bone before answering her. "Yeah. We totally had sex on the picnic table."

Sara's mouth dropped. "Seriously? I mean, that's what I was imagining, but still…are you okay? He's hanging with his club and you're waiting tables. Shouldn't you guys be talking or something?"

"How much time did you spend talking with Bone after you guys did it?" I asked her, feeling sick to my stomach. All that empowerment I'd felt on the outside was fading fast, now that he was back to flirting with the college girl groupies. Sara rolled her eyes.

"He didn't even offer me a ride home," she said. "And yet I keep working here."

"Where else are you gonna work?" I asked, shrugging. "We've got the bar, the grocery store and the gas station. The gas station's drug central and the grocery store's full up. This is our reality."

Bone came over with two pitchers, setting them on the pass-through. We both glared at him.

"What?" he asked.

"Fuck off," Sara snapped, walking away. Bone stared at me, eyes full of questions, and I offered him a tight smile.

"She's on the rag. We all are. Permanently."

"Jesus, what did I do?" he asked.

"Not a damned thing," I told him. "That's sort of the problem. Where are my drinks? Table seven wants their booze."

The rest of the night flew by.

I half expected Shade to up and leave with one of the college girls. That's what men did, or at least what the good ones did. The bad ones got you arrested while they robbed liquor stores. Instead he stuck around, waiting patiently as the bar cleared out and I finished cleaning up my tables.

As for me, I was conflicted. The sex had been good. Really good. I wanted more of it, and given the fact that Shade was still here, he did too. This was something I could wrap my head around.

What I couldn't wrap my head around was voluntarily letting another man in my life at this point, even casually.

One night won't kill you, Wonder Woman said, surprising me.

But I thought we hated men?

No, we hate being traded for motorcycles, she replied. *And with your track record, a one-night stand is the best bet. Doesn't mean it can't be a hell of a night, though. One time Batman and I—*

"You ride your bike?" Shade asked, his lips brushing my ear. He'd come up behind me, pinning me against the bar with his hands. Bone had already given the last call and the lights were up. Most of the customers were gone.

"I ride it every night," I said, still torn. "Don't worry—it has lights. Nobody's going to run me over."

"Leave it here," he said. I felt his breath against my cheek. Smelled him all around me. My legs shifted restlessly, remembering how he'd felt deep inside. "Come back to the clubhouse with me."

I knew I should say no. Tell him I had to watch my sister's kids tomorrow, but for once Hannah didn't need me. She had the day off. My Saturday was totally free until six that night, when my next shift started. We'd already had sex—the damage was done. Why shouldn't I have some fun along the way?

"Okay," I said slowly. I turned in his arms, determined to set some firm boundaries. Unfortunately, this meant my breasts were pushing up against his chest and his strong thighs brushed mine, which was distracting. "But there are a couple things you should know first."

"What?"

I took a deep breath.

You can do this, Wonder Woman reminded me.

"No offense, but I have bad taste in men," I said, staring at the little dip at the bottom of his throat. Shade was tall. Big, too. Muscular. There was no way to forget the difference in our sizes or how much stronger he was than me. Not up close like this. "Really bad taste in men. That's why I'm absolutely, positively not looking for another relationship. Rebel might've been my boyfriend, but I was very clear with him. We had no future together and that was the way I wanted it…and even that turned out to be too much. He asked me to do a favor for him and you know how it ended, so whatever we do, I'm not going to be your girlfriend or even your friend with benefits. This is strictly about sex. One night only, and we're using condoms this time. Oh, and a ride home. I need a ride home after the sex. But that's it."

Next to us a man snorted with laughter. I glanced over to find Dopey, his club brother, listening in. Delightful. I decided to ignore him, turning back to stare steadily at Shade's throat because I didn't quite trust myself to meet his eyes.

"I think that's the strangest thing any woman's ever said to me," Shade finally replied.

"I'm just being straight up. I know myself and I know what I don't need, and that's a man. They always cause trouble in my life. *Always*. History doesn't lie."

"Okay, then I'll be straight up, too," he replied. "I think you know this already, but I'm the national president of the Reapers MC. Technically I've got a home base—an apartment up in Moscow, at least for now—but I spend maybe eight, ten weeks a year there. The rest of the time I'm traveling, spending time with different chapters. These men are my brothers and I'll do anything for them. I don't have time for playing house with a woman or picking out china patterns. I just wanna fuck you again."

Nothing he said surprised me, but the words still caught me off guard. Even after my little speech, I still hadn't expected him to be so honest. Rebel hadn't been honest with me. Neither had Trevor or my dad or any of Mom's other husbands. Randy had lied his ass off to Hannah.

"All right, then," I said, hardly believing what I was doing.

Anticipation flared and I felt almost giddy as I looked up, finally meeting his gaze. "Let's do it. Let's go to your clubhouse and have one night of crazy monkey sex and absolutely not make any promises to each other."

Dopey started laughing again and Shade flipped him the bird, offering me a slow smile.

Riding through the darkness with Shade was amazing.

This time I didn't worry about whether I was holding him too tight or what might happen after we got there. I knew exactly what would be happening. We'd go to his weird little room in the bunkhouse and fuck like bunnies. So what if people gave me knowing looks and smirks? This time I wouldn't give a shit because I was in control.

When I'd ridden with him before, I'd wondered what he would feel like buried deep between my legs. I'd felt the hard muscles of his stomach and speculated.

Even had a few sex dreams.

The reality would be even better, which I knew for a fact because we'd already had sex. Me and him. Down and dirty. Fantastic, raunchy Sexual Intercourse with a capital "I" and zero strings attached.

I'd blow him off afterward like a gangster, because that's who I was.

A motherfucking *gangster.*

Well, more of a gangster/waitress hybrid, with a strong sense of responsibility, but still fairly badass as these things went. Not that I had any delusions—if I allowed myself even a hint of feeling toward Shade, he'd destroy me. This was clear. That was why I'd be keeping emotion out of it, a decision that was surprisingly liberating.

This is why men avoid relationships, I realized. *Because they're full of baggage and baggage is heavy.*

By the time we pulled up to the Reapers' clubhouse in Cranston, it was after four in the morning and everything was quiet. There were a few bikes parked out front, but not many.

"Where is everyone?" I asked Shade, who threw an arm around

my shoulders. Dopey unlocked the door for us.

"Home," he said. "Home or in bed. They'll be back this afternoon for a barbecue."

"Oh," I said, vaguely disappointed. The last time I'd been here the place was a full-on den of debauchery, and I'd been scared shitless they'd expect me to join in. Now I was ready to join and they weren't even here.

"Don't worry," Shade said, leaning over to give me a long, slow kiss. "You won't be bored. I promise."

We passed through the same greatroom I'd seen before, and then back through the courtyard. The fire was dead and the tents were gone. The lights were off in the bunkhouse, too. Dopey peeled off into one of the first rooms, clearly off duty for the night, and then we were there.

Shade's room.

Just me, him and the same bed I'd slept in before.

"So you don't really live here?" I asked. I already knew the answer, but now that we were actually about to do this thing, I felt weird and awkward. I needed to fill the silence.

"Nope," he answered, carefully taking off his leather vest and hanging it on a hook on the wall. "Got a place up north, remember?"

"So how long are you in Cranston, anyway?"

Shade turned to me, his mouth quirking. "Get over here."

"What?" I asked, suddenly nervous.

"Get your ass over here," he repeated, taking a step forward and sliding his hands down and around my waist. He tugged me gently into his body, the thick length of his cock digging into my stomach. That awesome chemistry between us kicked in again and the weirdness disappeared. I felt a tightening between my legs—a physical anticipation of the satisfaction I knew he'd give me. Reaching down, I slipped my hands under his shirt and then tugged it upward because I still hadn't seen his bare chest.

Shade held my gaze as my fingers slid along his skin. I found his nipples, grazing them lightly as his eyes darkened with desire. He had a Marine Corps tattoo over his pec and I traced it, wondering what his story was.

Does it matter? The two of you are just having sex. You aren't going to share stories, remember?

"Got that in Iraq," he said, as if reading my mind. "One tour. Didn't see any action for the first nine months, so I guess I had something to prove. Got the tattoo on leave and felt pretty badass about it. Then things fell to shit when I went back, and I learned that tattoos aren't what makes you a badass. Not even a little bit. Lot better men than me didn't make it."

"You surprise me," I said.

"How's that?"

"Usually guys want to brag about how tough they are."

"Usually girls want relationships," he countered. I blinked up at him and then smiled. Shade's eyes darkened and he leaned down, lips tracing the side of my neck.

"Guess I don't fit the stereotype," I whispered.

"Startin' to pick up on that." His hands slid into the waistband of my skirt, pushing it down along with my panties. I kicked them off. Shade reached around my hip and down between my legs from behind, finding my wet warmth waiting for him as he slowly backed me to the bed.

I fell onto it suddenly, bouncing as the big biker grinned, ripping his shirt over his head and then reaching for his fly. His cock sprang free and I saw it for the first time—*really* saw it. Long and hard and unusually thick around the middle. Damn, no wonder it felt like he'd fucked me deeper than Rebel ever did. The guy was hung.

"We're using a condom this time," I reminded him firmly. "Just in case you had any doubts."

"Hell, yes," Shade replied, kneeling down on the floor between my legs. He caught my hips, scooting me toward the edge of the bed, then draped my legs over his shoulders. *Wooohooo!* "Sorry I didn't earlier. Don't know what the fuck I was thinking."

"Both our faults," I acknowledged, sighing as his fingers spread me open, the heat of his breath hitting my clit like a tangible touch.

Then his tongue grazed my center and the whole world narrowed. His touch was sure, his tongue clever and quick. You know, like he was into it, not just trying to get me off or convince me to do the same for him. Nope. Shade traced my clit and then sucked it like he had all night, which I supposed he did. I don't know how long he kept it up, but it was long enough that I came once and nearly came again before he raised his head.

Moving up my body, he lifted my shirt and bra, pulling them off completely before taking my mouth. I tasted myself on his lips as he kissed me hard. Grabbing his ass, I dug my fingers into the tight muscles as he rubbed his cock against my center. The oral thing had been great but I wanted more. Now. Turning my head, I broke free from his kiss.

"Condom," I gasped, wondering where the hell I'd dropped my purse.

"Fuck, I almost forgot again," Shade muttered, shaking his head. "You got a magic pussy or something."

I laughed as he leaned over me, reaching across the bed toward the dresser, awkwardly pulling out one of the drawers. He grabbed a string of condoms, ripping open one of the packages. The slick rubber fell out and hit my face and I burst out laughing.

Shade started laughing too, and then I helped him roll the condom over his cock, giving it a couple pumps for good measure. Seconds later, he'd lined it up with my opening.

Then he thrust deep and I forgot everything else.

Chapter Thirteen

For the second time that week I woke up in the Reapers MC clubhouse. I wasn't sure what time we'd finally gone to sleep, but it was well after the sun came up. Holy shit, but Shade knew what he was doing in bed… Not only that, he gave pretty good post-sex snuggle for a one-night stand. Rolling over, I felt a hint of soreness between my legs, a glorious ache that reminded me just how many different ways he'd found to make me come.

Now he was gone.

I sat up slowly and looked around the room. It was every bit as faded and anonymous as I remembered it, like a hotel that rented by the hour. I'd had a really good time, but looking at the light outside, I knew it was over.

I should find my clothes and catch a ride home before I did something stupid to fuck it up. Something like telling him I didn't want it to end, because it'd been good. Too good. The last thing I needed was to fall for the guy—didn't matter how nice our snuggling felt.

Yours Truly was officially off the market.

I found my bra and tank top hanging on the edge of the dresser, where he'd tossed them. The skirt and panties were harder to locate, but I eventually discovered them under the bed, in a dried puddle of something very questionable.

I managed to brush the dust bunnies off the skirt, but no matter how much I shook the panties, I couldn't bring myself to put them on. I didn't know what that brown stuff on the floor was, but I was pretty sure I didn't want it touching my coochie.

Of course, that would leave me doing the walk of shame in a micro skirt and nothing else.

You should really keep extra panties in your purse, Wonder Woman suggested helpfully. *A girl never knows when she's going to need a fresh pair of star-spangled briefs.*

Well, I guess she would know.

I found my purse and dug out a brush, attacking my hair. I knew my makeup had to look like shit, but I could clean that up in the bathroom, wherever the hell it was. Then maybe I could borrow something to cover my ass and head home.

The door opened and Shade stepped in, holding a ceramic mug. He was fully dressed in jeans, shirt and leather Reapers' colors, and had clearly been awake for a while.

"Thought I'd let you sleep," he said, holding out the mug. Coffee, God love him.

"Thanks," I replied, feeling that same awkwardness from last night falling between us. He looked past me, his eyes catching on something. My bright pink panties, which I'd dropped on the bed. Shade raised a brow, questioning.

"They were down on the floor and it's icky," I admitted. "I didn't want to put them back on. I don't suppose you have anything I can borrow to wear home…?"

He took a step closer, into my space.

"Yeah, this isn't gonna work."

"What?"

"Give me the coffee."

"But I want the coffee."

"Give me the fuckin' coffee," he said, his voice a low growl. I handed it over. Shade lifted the mug and drank deep, throat moving as he emptied the cup. Holding my eyes, he dropped it. Then he reached out and caught me by the sides of my skirt, pulling me into his body. I had just a second to realize what he was doing before his hands were under my skirt, cupping my bare ass. Our mouths connected and he pushed me back onto the bed with a bounce. My hands reached for his jeans as he grabbed a fresh condom.

Then he was inside me again.

Half an hour later, I rolled over and stretched in satisfaction because who needed coffee with a dick like Shade's to wake you up? Leaning up on one elbow, I studied his body, rubbing my hand over his bare stomach. His skin was slightly darker than mine, with just enough tan to tell me he worked outside sometimes without a shirt, and his muscles were all lean and rippled. He could've been a model.

Maybe I should give the friends with benefits thing a try…

No! Bad Mandy! shouted Wonder Woman.

Shade caught me with his arm and tucked me into his side, oblivious to my mental battle for self-control.

"What's your plan for the day?" he asked.

"Heading home," I told him, because Wonder Woman was right. I was being a bad Mandy and I needed to behave myself. "I have to work tonight. What time is it, anyway?"

"Just after one," he said. "They're setting up for the barbecue outside. You should stick around for a while. You already know some of the club from the bar. Might as well get to know them a little better."

His eyes held mine steadily, his face unreadable.

"Um, wouldn't that be weird?" I asked, hating the fact that a small part of me was all excited because he wasn't ready for me to leave yet. "I thought we weren't doing anything like dating or whatever."

"It's not a date," he said, his voice relaxed. "It's hamburgers with a bunch of bikers. Beer. Maybe even some kids. It's a family event, at least until later tonight."

"Will Rebel's club be here?"

"Maybe. We invited the support clubs. Although it's not a mandatory event, so they aren't required to show up."

"About Rebel…"

Shade rolled me up onto his body, sliding his hands down to my butt and squeezing.

"Really like this ass of yours," he said. "Usually I go for the boobs, but with you it's a tough call. Let's not talk about your ex-boyfriend. I don't like thinkin' about him fuckin' this ass."

I stilled. What the hell was that supposed to mean?

"Just a second—" I said, pushing against his chest. Shade ignored my puny efforts, gripping me tighter. His cock twitched and I realized he was staring at my breasts. "No—stop! We aren't doing this anymore. First, this is a one-night stand and it's light outside. That means it's over. And not that it's any of your business, but Rebel didn't fuck my ass. We had a lot of fun together, but I've never actually done that and I don't like the idea of him going around talking about our sex life."

"How many one-night stands have you had?" Shade asked, his voice curious. I was too busy trying to wrap my head around the fact that Rebel had told Shade—of all people—that I was into butt sex to answer the question. Jesus. What a fucking douche.

"Mandy."

"What?"

"How many one-night stands?"

"Um, counting this one?" I asked, trying to focus. His hands were starting to wander, which made thinking even harder.

"Yeah."

"One," I admitted, wondering if he'd laugh at me.

Shade nodded, his face serious.

"I've had a lot more than one," he said. "Which means of the two of us, I'm the expert on random fucking. I know all the best practices and shit. And I'm tellin' you, buying a girl breakfast before taking her home is just the decent thing to do."

"Taking them out to breakfast probably makes it easier to get rid of them, too," I blurted out. Shade laughed.

"I'll plead the Fifth on that," he said, shifting me slightly to the side, casually raising a knee between my legs. One hand started up my back, his strong fingers finding my muscles and massaging them. It felt good. Really good. "Where I'm going with this is that we missed breakfast, but as a good one-night stand, I still owe you some food. Stick around for a burger before work. You can go to the barbecue, eat and have a good time without fucking up the one-night thing. Then I'll take you home in time for work."

I shifted against him, considering. Biker barbecues were fun, at least the ones I'd gone to with Rebel. And if I was going to keep working at the Pit, I'd have to get over seeing members of his club. Speaking of…

"Okay, I know this is crazy, but you didn't kill Rebel, did you?"

Shade burst out laughing this time, his entire body shaking. My face burned and I groaned, feeling stupid. Of course he hadn't killed him. Not over something as stupid as a girl.

Technically it would've been the $500 and not you, Wonder Woman reminded me.

Bitch.

"No, I didn't kill him," Shade said, still laughing. "I may have swung by his place with some of the brothers and shared my feelings about what he tried to pull, but that's it. His own people were smart enough to kick him out before the Reapers had to take action. You're the one who destroyed his truck, not me. Last I heard, he was catching a bus to Boise."

I buried my face against his neck, wondering if I could just make myself disappear.

"What, you can't tell me you regret doing it?" he asked. I shook my head.

"No, but the guys in his club—you're sure they aren't pissed at me? Amelia said it was okay, but what if someone gets me alone and wants revenge?"

"One, you've been watching too much *Sons of Anarchy,*" Shade said, and while he wasn't laughing out loud anymore, I could tell he was still amused. "This isn't a violent, bloody revenge barbecue. It's the peaceful kind, where you eat burgers, drink some beer and hang out. But even if it was, it wouldn't be about you. It was never about you, babe. This was a thing between Rebel and the Reapers. His club knows that, which is why he's out bad. Dishonorable discharge."

Pushing back up, I stared at him, embarrassment fading back into outrage. "Of course it's about me. *He tried to trade me for part of a motorcycle.* A hunk of metal. He had no right to do that, and that's very much about me. You're just the guy he tried to trade me to."

"No."

"Yes!"

"Nope. That's not how it works," Shade said, sliding his hand up into my hair. "It was about a member of a support club lying to the national president of the Reapers. He tried to cheat me out of five hundred bucks by promising something he didn't own. We can't let guys like Rebel get away with that shit. Wouldn't matter what it was about, the principle's the same."

"There are so many things wrong with that statement that I don't even know where to start. I…I literally can't figure out what I want to argue with you about because it's all wrong. All of it."

"It's how our world works," he said, rubbing up and down my lower back. He might've been trying to soothe me but my thoughts were spinning too fast. "There's good and bad. Part of the good is that when you belong to someone in a club, it's not just his job to protect you, it's the whole club's. I'd die for Dopey's old lady and I don't even like the bitch. He's my brother, though, and she's his property. It is what it is."

I laid my head down on his shoulder, fuming. Fucking stupid men, ruining everything again. Except Shade hadn't actually ruined anything for me. Yeah, he'd taken a night with me in trade, but I guess technically it was acceptable within the rules of the club. He'd definitely thought I was on board with it. More importantly, he'd stopped when he learned that I'd been set up.

I raised my head again.

"Is that really true? What you said about Dopey's old lady?"

"Naw," Shade said, smiling. "I like her okay."

"Seriously," I said, rolling my eyes. "You'd die for some woman you hardly know, just 'cause she's with this guy who's part of your club?"

Shade's smile faded and his face turned serious. "Yeah, it's really true. I'd die for her because Dopey's my brother and that's what it means to be a Reaper."

"Rebel and his club aren't like that, are they?" I asked, the magnitude of his words finally sinking in.

"No, they aren't. They're great people and they'd do a hell of a lot for each other, but at the end of the day they aren't an MC. And that's perfectly fine—this life isn't for everyone."

"But it's for you."

Shade nodded. "Yeah, it's for me."

"Okay, then," I told him.

"So, you wanna go eat burgers with some guys I'd die for and their women?" Shade asked. "I'm not trying to influence you either way, but I hear there's gonna be cake."

"Well, if they're serving cake, I guess it's only polite," I replied. "I wouldn't want to fuck up my very first one-night stand by being rude."

"Fantastic. I'll go see if I can find you something to wear. Let's go."

With that he gave my bare ass a smack. I shoved at him and he rolled me over, kissing me deep.

After that we needed another condom.

Shade

The barbecue was a mixture of fun and sheer torture because Mandy's almost-naked ass was hanging out the whole damned time, taunting me.

I liked having her around, but I wasn't a big fan of the looks she was getting. I hadn't been specific enough when I asked McClane's old lady, Pepper, to find her something to wear. It wasn't Pepper's fault that she was a couple sizes smaller than Mandy, but I'd never seen a pair of cut-offs cover less skin. The fact that I knew she wasn't wearing anything under them wasn't helping. Throw in the push-up bra, and my new girl might as well be in a bikini.

Not that she realized I'd claimed her, although everyone else at the fucking picnic sure as shit did. Wasn't sure how long we'd last, but while she was sleepin' with me, she wouldn't be sleepin' with anyone else. No fuckin' way.

One-night stand?

Like hell.

She'd be back in my bed, and damned soon, too.

"Just got word, boss," said Dopey, sitting down next to me at the picnic table. He held a beer in one hand and a disposable cell in the other. "The brothers down south said they got eyes on Rebel.

Want to know if we're done with him."

"We'll see how he settles in," I replied. "They can keep an eye on him, make sure he understands that going out bad isn't a temporary state of being. He's dead to the MC world."

"Oh, I think he figured that out," Dopey said, offering me a feral smile. "I thought you showed restraint, all things considered. None of the damage was permanent."

I shrugged. "Doing more could've caused trouble for Mandy. Wasn't necessary, which is a fuckin' pity. I'd have loved to slit his throat."

"Your girl seems to be doing all right for herself," Dopey said, nodding toward a gaggle of women clustered near the food tables. Mandy might've been nervous about sticking around, but she'd managed to find a place for herself. She had an energy, a sense of busy-ness that I'd noticed before. I'd figured it was related to her work as a waitress. Now I saw there was more to it. She didn't like sitting around or waiting for someone else to do the work. She'd volunteered to help with the food as soon as I officially introduced her to the old ladies, and not in a showy way. I'd caught several approving looks shared between Pepper and Jen, Dopey's old lady.

They liked her.

Rebel's club liked her, too. I'd been telling the truth when I'd said that it wasn't about her—it really wasn't. But if they'd only been tolerating her for his sake, they wouldn't be so friendly toward her now that he was gone. Mandy might've joined the biker community by hooking up with Rebel, but more than one man here would be looking to pin her down when I cut her loose. I saw the way their eyes followed her, and I didn't like it. Didn't like it one damned bit.

Mandy turned to find me staring at her. I raised my beer, and she started across the courtyard.

"Hey, there!" she said when she reached the table. I swung one leg over the bench and caught her hand, pulling her down to sit in front of me.

"You havin' fun?" I asked. She twisted her head to smile at me.

"Yeah, I really am. You know, I always had a good time with the bikers. It was only—"

She stopped talking abruptly, her face going red.

"What?" I asked.

"It's stupid," she replied, shaking her head.

"Tell me."

"Promise you won't laugh?"

"Promise I won't make promises I can't keep," I told her. She shoved me playfully, then took a deep breath, glancing quickly at Dopey. The man was pretending not to listen. Poorly.

"Go away," I told him.

"Jen's gonna be pissy that I didn't get the good gossip," he muttered, and I made a whipping noise, pretending to crack one at him. He laughed and flipped me off, heading toward the keg. Mandy waited until he was out of earshot before speaking again.

"Okay, I was always sort of freaked out whenever the Reapers were around. Especially you," she admitted. It didn't really surprise me—we had that effect on a lot of people. Still, it took guts to admit it. "The way you were always watching me. And you kept trying to get me to…well, you know."

"Fuck me," I said. "I was tryin' to get you to fuck me. And see? I was right—it was fantastic. And we aren't scaring you today, are we?"

"Um, I mean you're still a bunch of big, intimidating guys," she said. "But you've been good to me. You know, aside from the whole renting me for five hundred bucks thing."

"Hey, it worked for me," I replied, wrapping my arms around her waist. "In the end, I got to fuck you. Mission accomplished."

Mandy tugged at my hands, pretending to be pissed, but she wasn't trying very hard. Then I kissed her neck and she relaxed back into me, dropping her head against my shoulder.

"You're a horrible man and I shouldn't be letting you do this," she muttered. "But you're really good at it."

I slid my hand up and under her tank top, finding her tit and giving it a squeeze. Mandy squeaked and smacked at me again, this time for real, and I started laughing.

"You can't stand being nice for even a minute, can you?" she asked, twisting her head back around. "People can see us."

"Baby, wearin' those shorts with your legs wide open, it's not your boobs they're lookin' at."

She looked down between her legs, and while I couldn't see the horror on her face, it wasn't too hard to imagine it. Mandy obviously had no clue how much they were riding up. The strip of cloth between her legs covered about as much as a thong.

She all but spun on the bench, bringing her legs together, and I burst out laughing for real. She glared at me, then flipped me off, which made me laugh louder.

"You're such an asshole!" she hissed. "And it's getting late. I need to go home and get ready for work."

I wanted to tell her to blow it off, but I'd already tried that last night and she'd shot me down. Mandy took her job damned seriously. I wasn't used to that—women jumped to kiss my ass, no matter where I went. Some of it was looks, I knew this.

More of it was the patch and the title.

The Reapers were badass motherfuckers and I was their president. The job came with many responsibilities, but the pussy was a serious perk.

"Okay, I'll take you home," I said, and I caught a flicker of disappointment on Mandy's face. Someone wasn't as eager to end our night together as she insisted… She sighed, nodding her head.

"Home," she repeated. "I'll go grab my purse and meet you out front. I want to say good-bye to a couple people first."

"Sure thing," I said, watching her semi-exposed ass twitch as she hustled back over to the girls. That's when it hit me.

She'd just given me an order. Holy shit. I sat back, thinking about it. Couldn't remember the last time someone had tried telling me what to do, and now this little slip of nothing waitress was treating me like a Goddamn cab driver.

Fucking hell.

She was worth more than five hundred bucks, just for that alone.

Chapter Fourteen

Mandy

Here I was again—riding home with Shade, although this time it was bittersweet.

I'd had a good time with him. A great time, actually. So what if the thought of seeing him used to terrify me? That was back when I only knew scary (but sexy) Shade. Now I knew fun (even sexier) Shade, and somehow the two seemed to have settled into a balance that I really liked.

I didn't want him to drop me off at my trailer and then say good-bye forever.

Even worse, I didn't want to watch him hooking up with other girls at the Pit and have to pretend it didn't bother me, because it would. This…this was why it'd been stupid to give in to temptation and spend the night with him. Men were a slippery slope, one that started with the most innocent of glances and ended with me handcuffed in the back of a police car.

So I savored our ride home together but also steeled myself to say good-bye to him. I'd be casual and flippant. Gangster. No big deal. If Wonder Woman could do it, so could I.

Of course, I wasn't an Amazonian demi-goddess. I was just a waitress…

Shut up, Wonder Woman said. *Do you know how many heroic waitresses there are? A few years ago, the waitresses at a Denny's restaurant in Coeur d'Alene recognized an armed serial killer with a captive child, then stalled him until the police showed up! You telling me those women didn't have courage?*

Wait, what? Whoa… I had absolutely no memory of ever hearing or reading anything about this, so how the hell had my subconscious inserted it into an imaginary conversation with an Amazonian princess?

Holy shit. Was Wonder Woman real?

Jesus Christ, don't be ridiculous, Wonder Woman snapped. *Of course I'm not real. You're talking to yourself, nitwit.*

God. I was literally going crazy, on top of everything else. I tightened my hold on Shade and watched the road fly by under our wheels, trying very, very hard not to think of anything at all.

Thankfully, I'd managed to pull myself together and was braced to give Shade his casual good-bye when we reached Violetta. I was holding steady right up until we turned down the road and crossed the railroad tracks onto the flat. That's when Hannah's trailer came into view.

There was a sheriff's patrol car parked out front.

My nails dug into Shade's stomach, hard enough that he realized something was wrong. He passed the house, continuing down the street and then turning the corner to swing back around the grain elevator. There—safely hidden by the massive structure—he killed the big Harley engine.

Abrupt silence filled the air.

"I really like the way you scratch your nails down my back during sex," Shade said after a long pause. "But it's a hell of a lot less sexy when you're trying to claw out my stomach. Wanna let go so we can talk this out?"

"Oh, I'm sorry," I said, unclenching my fingers through will alone. Then I swung my leg over the bike. "Thanks so much for the ride. I can just walk home from here, no need to—"

Shade's hand shot out, catching my arm, forcing me to face him.

"Yeah, that's not gonna happen yet," he said. I stared down at the big fingers, wishing I'd been faster. Shade was strong—no way I'd be getting away from him now. "Why are you scared of cops? I understood why things were tense the other day. You didn't know why he was there and we'd just gone through the shit with Rebel. But you know damned well that Heath Andrews is at your house today 'cause he's into your sister. You don't need to be afraid of him. What gives?"

"Does it really matter?" I said, sighing as I looked at him. Really looked at him. God, I could hardly believe I'd slept with this guy. Shade was all badass and sunglasses and hair that'd been swept in the wind. I was just small town white trash with a good push-up bra. "It was just a one-night stand. Why do you care?"

Shade shook his head slowly, running his tongue along his bottom lip.

"Pull your head out of your ass, Mandy. This is not a one-night stand. I bought you a fucking phone and I introduced you to my friends. You came and ate burgers with us. What the fuck kind of one-night stand doesn't end until five o'clock in the afternoon?"

"But you said…breakfast…"

Shade cocked a brow, and I closed my eyes, realizing I'd been deluding myself. I wasn't a total moron. Shade didn't buy girls breakfast, and he sure as shit didn't hang out with them all day once the sex part was over.

This might not be a relationship, but it wasn't a typical one-night stand, either.

"I'm on probation," I blurted out.

"No shit," Shade said slowly, obviously startled. "What for?"

"Technically, I was an accessory to an attempted robbery, but then I pled down to a misdemeanor in stupidity," I said, staring at his bike's air-brushed gas tank. There was a picture of a pinup girl, like on a World War II airplane. It was good. Really good.

"You wanna elaborate on what happened?"

"Here's the thing," I said, looking back up at him and biting my lip. "It's the curse of the McBride women. I told you—we pick bad men. My mom got hitched five times, and not one of them stuck. She married the last one when we lived in Spokane. Hannah was nineteen and I was seventeen. One night he and Mom went out and they never came back, because he'd gotten drunk and crashed the car into the river."

"I'm really sorry, babe," Shade said, reaching his hand around the back of my neck, giving it a squeeze. I liked that. Supportive without the expectation that I was going to collapse in a puddle of tears. I'd survived way too much to fall apart behind a grain elevator.

"Thanks," I replied, pushing the memories away. "Anyway, so that was that. We bummed around for a while and then I met a guy in Missoula and decided he was Mr. Right, so I married him. His name was Trevor. I'm telling you—never trust a guy named Trevor. He had this other friend named Trevor and they were both shady as fuck."

"I'll keep that in mind."

I smiled grimly. "Yeah, you do that. Anyway, Trevor wasn't the greatest but it wasn't like my standards were that high. I'd had a few boyfriends, but nothing serious. Nobody ever stuck around. But Trevor did. He latched on to me like a suckerfish. Anyway, I was working full time while he was going to college. Then one day he and his friend Robert and the other Trevor decided to start this business. You know, he was going to make his fortune and all that. In computers. Told me I wasn't smart enough to understand."

Shade's hand tightened against my neck. "Sounds like a real winner."

"You could say that. What he was really getting into was drugs. All our money kept disappearing, but every time I talked to him about it, he had a good explanation. His laptop was broken, or his student loan hadn't come through.

"I knew he wasn't sober, but I had no clue how bad it really was. Then one night we had a fight because he wanted to go to the liquor store. I kept telling him he was drunk already and we should stay home. He wouldn't, so I insisted on driving him. I figured they wouldn't sell him anything, but that's not what he was there for. Somehow, he'd decided it would be a great idea to rob the place. With a butter knife, because my life's a fucking joke, you know?"

"A butter knife?" Shade asked, raising a brow.

"Yup," I said, knowing it sounded like a bad joke. Unfortunately, it was a felony-level bad joke. "A *plastic* one. He wasn't a very good robber."

"Jesus," Shade said. "There's a lot of dumbass criminals out there, but seriously—sounds like Trevor boy was a new level."

"Yeah, well, who's stupider—Trevor or me, because I'm the who one fell for his shit. Then I got arrested as his accomplice. I had no damned idea what was going on when the cops pulled up. I thought they were just trying to say hello when they knocked on my window. Anyway, I spent three nights in jail before I found someone to bail me out. Things went downhill from there, obviously. Trev was so fucked up that he could hardly talk, but somehow he managed to tell them that the whole thing was my idea. Apparently I wasn't just his getaway driver—I was his butter knife supplier."

Shade gave a choked cough, and I cocked my head at him.

"It's okay to laugh," I said, and his lip twitched. Other than that, he managed to hold it in, which I appreciated. "Everyone else did. Then the prosecutor decided to take pity on me and offer a plea bargain. I got a misdemeanor and six months' probation. I was a good girl for the first three months so they dropped my supervision. I had to petition to move to Violetta, of course, but they were really decent about it."

"And then you met Rebel."

"Less than two weeks after I got here. You saw how that ended. Anyway, that's why I get nervous when I see cops. You never know when one of them is going to arrest you for something you didn't even know you did...and if I *do* get caught doing anything, I could go to jail. Have you ever been to jail? It sucks."

Shade nodded, and I remembered the rumors I'd heard about him. Of course he'd been to jail.

"I've been arrested several times. Never convicted," he told me. "And you're right—it's not pleasant. But it's not the end of the world, either. I've got brothers serving hard time inside, so that gives me some perspective. How much longer do you have?"

"Four more weeks."

"That's not bad at all," he said. "You got any special plans for afterward?"

Right. Special plans, because I can afford to do all kinds of crazy stuff as a waitress. You know, in all my free time, when I'm not watching my sister's kids in our luxurious trailer. I sighed, shaking my head. "You're really lucky, you know that?"

Shade sat back on his bike, studying me.

"Yeah, I think I'm a lucky enough guy, but I'm not quite sure what it has to do with the conversation."

"You get to travel," I told him, frustrated. "In a few weeks or a month or whatever you'll leave this place. You'll go see things and do things, and for some reason you seem to have enough money to live on without taking a shitty job waiting tables."

Shade snorted. "Mandy, you don't wanna know how I get my money."

"Let me guess—it's bad?" I asked, rolling my eyes. "I'm starting to think I'm genetically incapable of being attracted to a good guy. No offense."

"None taken," he replied, offering a slow smile. "I'm not a good man. But I'm not a man who'll drag you down into the dirt, either. Or let you get caught up in club business. The Reapers have been around for a long time and we're real good at taking care of our people. I'm not sayin' I'll never need a getaway car, but if I do, I sure as shit won't trick my woman into driving it."

God, how was he so sexy when he was saying such terrible things? And that knowing, naughty look in his eyes… It wasn't fair.

"This is crazy," I said, trying hard not to smile back at him. "I need to get to work and you need to go do whatever it is that you do that may or may not involve getaway cars. I'm sorry that I was weird about Heath's car. I know he's just there to see Hannah. He's probably even a good guy. I overreacted and it was stupid."

"I've asked around about him," Shade said, his voice serious this time. "And he *is* a good guy. A real good guy. Good enough that he won't play ball with us, if it makes you feel better."

"It actually does," I admitted, then my purse buzzed. Pulling out my phone, I found a message from Hannah.

Hannah: Are you ever coming home? i saw you drive by. Heath just stopped by to say hi

Me: Yeah will be there soon. Sorry. It felt weird seeing him there and I guess i panicked

Hannah: He's a good guy.

Shade must've been reading the messages upside down, because he laughed.

Me: so i hear. coming home soon

I looked at Shade, stiffening my spine.

"Okay, so you've heard the story, we've finished our one-night stand, we've finished the bonus barbecue, and now it's time for me to go to work," I said. "It's been fun."

"Great. I'll wait while you get ready and run you over to the Pit," Shade told me, patting the back of his bike. "Hop on. I can't stick around tonight because I gotta go back to the clubhouse, but I'll be in touch. Bone will change your work schedule if I need him to."

"Um, weren't you listening?" I asked. "I have to stay single. Otherwise, you'll destroy my life. It's my destiny."

Shade reached out, hooking his fingers into my waistband, then pulled me close.

"I didn't ask you to marry me," he said seriously, catching and holding my gaze. "And I promise, I have no plans to. But we aren't done fuckin'."

Oh, God, I wished that could be true. But there'd been my dad, Trevor, Rebel, Randy and so many others. "I'm sorry, but I just can't afford to take the chance on a guy right now."

Shade studied me, then nodded. "Okay, so we'll just have another one-night stand."

"But they're only one night—that's the definition."

"Yeah, and they don't include afternoon barbecues, but we managed to survive one, didn't we? So we'll just fuck again. No relationships. I promise."

It really would be nice. And I was already setting Future Me up for a win by finishing out my probation.

Yes, you are, said Wonder Woman approvingly. *Future You is a very lucky girl.*

"All right. We can have sex again, but there won't be any relationship bullshit. You need a getaway driver, call someone else. Dopey. You should call Dopey. He's a decent guy, even if he is nosy."

"I'll be sure to tell him that," Shade said, cracking a smile.

Chapter Fifteen

I slept in the next morning, or at least as much as I could with three little girls sitting on me while they watched cartoons. It was Sunday and Hannah was making pancakes.

That meant she wanted to ask me a favor. I had a massive weakness for pancakes and we both knew it.

Just to spite her, I pretended not to notice until she literally waved them under my nose. Then it was all over because she'd put in chocolate chips. Whatever she wanted me to do, she felt strongly about it—those were the big guns. Half an hour later I sat at the counter, watching as she dried the dishes. Usually, whoever cooked didn't have to clean, which raised the stakes even more.

"Okay, spit it out," I said, waiting until she was done. That way if I told her no she couldn't stick me with kitchen duty, because that's what sisters do to each other.

"What?" Hannah asked, all innocence.

"Just tell me what the favor is. You wouldn't have pulled out the chocolate chips if wasn't a big deal to you… But it's also something that you think I might say no to, which means it's technically optional. Otherwise you wouldn't bother sucking up so hard. It's about Heath, isn't it?"

Hannah dropped the innocent act and put both hands on the counter, leaning across the faded laminate toward me.

"He asked me out on a date," she said in a hushed tone. "Like, a *real* date. Oh, don't look at me like that. It wasn't the police department's fault you got arrested and thrown into jail. They were just there to finish what Trevor started. And Heath is cute—really cute. Not only that, he's stable and nice and doesn't do drugs. He's a volunteer baseball coach, for God's sake. What more do you want?"

"I hate it when you're all reasonable and expect me to be reasonable, too. It's not fair."

"Whatever. Will you watch the girls or not?" she asked, crossing her arms and glaring at me.

"Ha! I knew you couldn't keep up the nice act," I replied, sticking out my tongue. She stuck hers out back at me. "But yeah, I'll watch the kids. When?"

"Tonight," she said. "It's the only day this week that neither of us have to work. More like this afternoon, really. He wants to go on a picnic, maybe watch the sunset from the butte."

"Bullshit. He wants to go park somewhere and make out with you."

Hannah blushed fiercely as I waved my finger in disapproval.

"Men are the enemy, remember?"

"Says the girl who came home at five in the afternoon, delivered by a strange biker. Don't be such a hypocrite. Anyway, I never said anything about staying away from men. That was you. Just because things didn't work out with Randy doesn't mean they can't with someone else."

"This kind of attitude might be why Mom was married five times," I pointed out.

"Well, if she'd stuck with my dad, she'd never have met yours, and then I wouldn't have a sister," Hannah replied. "It's just one date. Will you let me have this? Please?"

I sighed melodramatically and then nodded at her. "Okay, you can go out with Heath… But I'll expect you back by dark or I'll have to ground you."

Hannah gave the children a quick glance to make sure they were still watching TV, then flipped me off. My phone buzzed before I could retaliate.

Shade: Hey—you busy today? Another one-night stand might be nice… Technically we never finished the first one. You didn't get breakfast

I looked at Hannah, holding the phone up so she could read it.

"Please don't bail on me!" she said, eyes wide. "I'll do your laundry."

"I'm listening," I told her, although we both knew I'd keep my promise no matter what. We only had each other to rely on, so we had to be damned reliable.

"Um…and I'll sleep on the couch. You can have the whole bedroom to yourself tonight."

"You're just saying that so you can sneak in super late and I won't know."

"Well, yeah."

I snorted, turning back to my phone.

Me: Sorry. My stupid sister wants to go on a stupid date and get laid by the stupid cop. I need to babysit

This was where—in the John Hughes movie version of my life—Shade would've offered to come over and help watch the kids. He'd bring a pizza. Then they'd take their naps and we'd kiss across a coffee table or something.

Of course, that's the kind of thing that boyfriends did.

Shade: Ok. You work tomorrow night?

Me: Dont know. Bone does the schedule on sunday afternoons.

Shade: I'll talk to him. Make sure he leaves some time for us

Me: I need those shifts to pay the bills. Keep your nose out of it. Your just a guy I had sex with

Shade: Keep telling yourself that. I'll talk to bone

"Looks like lover boy wants more of that sweet McBride action," Hannah said, sticking her finger in her mouth and poking the side of her cheek out with her tongue in the universal symbol for blow job.

"You're disgusting."

She leaned closer. "You're horny—I can smell it on you. Just don't forget to make him work for it."

"I'm not making him work for anything. It really was just a one-night stand. I'm sworn off men, remember?"

"Yeah, right," Hannah said. "Sell your shit to someone else. I saw the way you two looked at each other when he brought you home. You're not done yet."

Ignoring her, I stared down at Shade's message, trying to decide how to answer… Should I take a stand or just wait and see what happened? I waited for Wonder Woman to speak up and tell me, but she wasn't talking.

Fuck it.

I'd let it go and see what happened. Future Me was a smart girl. She'd figure it out.

Sure enough, Hannah and Heath hadn't come home by the time it started getting dark. I'd taken the kids down to the park after dinner and run them hard, then threw all three of them into the tub together and read them the Berenstain Bears while they splashed around.

A second bear story got us through bedtime. I tucked them in, then grabbed a beer and the TV remote, hoping Hannah was having a good time. She was right about one thing—Heath really did seem like one of the good ones.

He'd brought flowers when he picked her up.

For *me*.

Said he wanted to thank me for watching the kids so he could take her out. I'm not saying I melted into a little puddle of warm goo or anything, but a girl's just not natural if she doesn't love fresh flowers.

I'd made it through both my second beer and a second episode of the Kardashians when my phone buzzed.

Shade: Hows it going?
Me: I'm drinkng alone in the dark and watching the kardashians.
Shade: ouch

Me: No kidding. They don't even work for a living. Why do they get to wear shiny stuff and travel all over while I have to wait tables?

Shade: Well the fact that the $500 I gave you as a tip is still sitting in Bones office might be part of the problem. If your goal is money then you're doing it wrong

He made a good point. I looked around the room, thinking of all the things we could do with five hundred bucks. I'd start with a new couch, I decided. I could probably find one on Craigslist for less than two hundred. Preferably one that didn't still smell faintly of the disgusting AXE body spray Randy loved so much.

We could really use a new table, too. Or a new TV—ours had a blue band on the left side, running right through the picture. I took another drink. If I had to be honest, everything in the whole damned house needed replacing. The girls had a decent bed, of course. And we kept it as clean as we could. But the trailer was old and faded and there was a strange smell in the bathroom that never quite went away…

To hell with new furniture—we needed a new house. Five hundred bucks wouldn't make a dent. Depressing.

Me: I'm bored. What are you doing?

Shade: I'm at the bar. Bone has been glaring at me all night because I told him you can't work tomorrow

Me: We already covered this. I'm going in to work. New topic

Shade: What are you wearing?

Me: Clothes. You?

Shade: I'm in a bar. What do you think?

Me: A fancy dress with lots and lots of ribbons

Shade: Sure, it's red with black lace. And underneath it is super sexy lingerie. Now tell me what's under your clothes…

I snickered. Had to give him credit—the guy never gave up. Pushing myself off the couch, I went over to the girls' door and peeked in. All three of them were sound asleep, the pink glow of the night-light bathing their little faces. Then I walked into the kitchen and grabbed another beer before going into Hannah's room. She'd said I could have the bed that night and I planned to take her up on it.

Setting the beer down, I unbuttoned my jeans and pushed them down, grabbing a pair of sleep shorts out of the laundry basket. Then I slid my arms into my shirt and reached around behind to unhook the bra. Feeling lazy, I let it fall to the floor before climbing into the bed and propping myself up against the pillows.

The phone buzzed again.

Shade: Waiting

Me: I just took off my bra and got into bed

Shade: Tell me more

Me: About what?

Shade: Tell me what else you took off or I'll come and see for myself. I could be there in five minutes

Oh, shit. Would he really come here? Of course he would. Shade didn't do the whole boundaries thing. He didn't do shame, either. He wasn't the kind of guy to show up with pizza while you're babysitting, but he'd make a booty call after the kids went to sleep. I'd bet money on it.

Me: Bad idea

Shade: Talk to me then

Me: I'm wearing sleep shorts and a T-shirt. Not sexy at all

Shade: Nope, definitely not sexy. You should take them off. Much sexier

I laughed despite myself, then took a deep drink of the beer. Warmth settled into my stomach, and I scooted lower into the bed.

Me: I'm leaving them on, but I'm sliding my hand down into my shorts.

Shade: Touch yourself. You wet?

A tingle of awareness rushed through me. I shivered.

Me: where does phone sex fall in terms of one night stands?

Shade: Phone sex doesn't count. But think how much fun it'd be if you didn't have to type everything. Call me.

Calling was probably a bad idea, I thought.

He's right, though, Wonder Woman said. *Phone sex doesn't count. Everyone knows that.*

Hmmm...she probably knew what she was talking about, right? I mean, she was a demi-goddess. I killed the rest of my beer, found his name in my contact list and hit the dial button.

"Mandy," he said, that low, gritty voice of his sending shivers through me just like it had the first time I'd heard it. "Wasn't sure you'd call."

I heard the noise of the bar in the background, but it was getting softer. Like he was walking away.

"Where are you?" I asked.

"Just stepped outside," he said. "Heading around the back of the building. I like the picnic table there. Fond memories."

My cheeks grew warm. It *was* a nice table—hadn't left a single splinter in my ass, even though we'd been going at it hardcore. God, I was such a slut.

"So, you never answered the question," he said.

"What question?"

"Are you wet for me?"

I slid my hand down, under the covers and into my pants.

"Yeah, I am."

"Christ, I'd love to be there eating you out right now. You got a real cute little clit—did you know that? If I was there, I'd start by flicking it with my tongue. Use your fingers and tell me what it feels like."

I closed my eyes, relaxing back as I touched the little nub.

"It's slippery," I said, sliding from my clit down to my opening, then swiping back up again. My lower body tightened, and while it wasn't as good as him being there, just the sound of his voice made me hot.

"You're tight," he told me. "I knew it'd be good, but when I first got inside, I thought I might die. You were so damned tight.

Squeezing me."

"I love the feel of it…"

"Of what?" he said. "I want all the details."

"Your cock," I said hesitantly, fingers moving faster as the tension started to build. "When you first—"

"Auntie Mandy?" Callie stuck her head through door. I jerked my hand out of my pants, heart racing.

"What is it, baby?" I asked, fumbling with the phone.

"I found something in the bathroom," she replied, turning on the light. My eyes flooded from the sudden glare. I blinked as the little girl walked across the small room, holding something out to me. A baggie. "It's one of Daddy's secrets."

My eyes widened and I sat up, forgetting all about Shade. Callie handed it to me, looking scared. The bag held a handful of white crystal rocks. Holy shit… Was that what I thought it was? Meth. That was *meth*. Had to be. I was holding a bag of Goddamn *meth*—a bag delivered by a five-year-old child.

"Motherfucker…" I whispered, and Callie frowned.

"That's a Daddy word," she told me. "Mommy says we should never say it."

I raised my eyes from the bag to look at her, feeling sick. "You said this was Daddy's secret. Does that mean Mommy doesn't know about it?"

Callie squirmed and looked away. "I'm not supposed to tell, but Daddy said that if I ever found more of it, I needed to give it to him right away. Not Mommy. You know, so the twins don't try to eat it again. But he's not here and I'm worried. He said it could kill them."

Taking a deep breath, I set the bag carefully on the side table. That was when I realized the phone was still on. I reached for it and hung up on Shade. Hopefully he hadn't heard anything, but if he had, I'd deal with it later. Right now I needed to focus on Callie.

"It's good that you told someone," I said slowly. "You said that you're supposed to tell him if you find more so the twins don't try to eat it again. Does that mean they've tried to eat it before, baby?"

Callie's eyes started to water and she looked away.

Fuck. This was real. This was really happening. Fucking fuck *fuck!*

"It's okay to talk to me," I said, catching her little hand. It was cold, with just a hint of a tremor. The poor kid was terrified. "This is important, Callie. Talking about it is the right thing to do. You know how there are good secrets and bad secrets?"

"Yes, like people touching my privates," she whispered. I wrapped my arms around her, pulling her up and onto my lap.

"This is one of those bad secrets, baby girl. Even if Daddy said not to talk about it, he was wrong. You need to tell me everything, so we can be sure you and your sisters are safe. When have you seen something like this before?"

"Sometimes Daddy and his friends…" she whispered. "When Mommy's at work, sometimes they had stuff like this. And one time I found the twins playing with some. They thought it was candy but I yelled at them and they stopped. Daddy ran in and took it away from them. He said not to tell Mommy, that it was important because we'd all get in really big trouble."

That mother*fucking* asshole.

I couldn't believe this was happening. I knew Randy was scum, but leaving *meth* where his babies could eat it? What the fuck? And how the hell had Hannah let things get this far?

"And did you ever share the secret with Mommy?" I asked her, wondering what I'd do if she said yes. If my sister had knowingly allowed this to continue… No. She wouldn't. Not Hannah. She'd slit his throat before she let him put the girls in this kind of danger. I *had* to believe that.

"No," Callie said, sniffing. Holding her tight, I started rocking her softly, rubbing her hair. "I didn't want Daddy to yell at me. It was really scary and his friends were mean, too. One of them made me sit on his lap. Then he took away my Lambie. He said I'd only get it back if I kept the secret. I'm scared he'll come back, Auntie Mandy."

"It's okay," I reassured her, even though it wasn't. It wasn't okay even a little bit. I couldn't even wrap my head around how *not okay* it was, but I had to stay calm. Otherwise she'd panic. "Just tell me—besides that time and today…have you ever seen it any other times?"

Callie nodded her head, then started sobbing. I cradled her little head against my shoulder, rocking harder. It hurt. It hurt so bad to think of her going through this alone.

I wanted to kill him.

This wasn't just me being angry, I realized. I literally wanted Randy *dead*. Then maybe the girls would be safe.

Callie cried harder, sniffling loudly as I rocked her harder.

"It's okay, baby girl," I said, even though that was a big fat lie. It wasn't okay and it never would be. "You cry all you want. You're safe now. I'll never let them scare you again."

"You promise?" she said. I kissed her head.

"Yeah, sweet girl. I promise."

"Pinkie promise?" She pulled away, holding one tiny, trembling finger up for me. I wrapped my own around it, catching and holding her gaze.

"I promise on my pinkie that I will never, ever let those men scare you again."

Callie nodded slowly, then laid her head back down on my shoulder. I rubbed her back until the tears started to slow, kissing the top of her head every few seconds. It was warm and just a little sweaty. She still smelled like baby. This wasn't right. It wasn't *fair*.

"Are you going to tell Daddy?" she finally asked. "He'll be mad. Really mad. He said that if I told anyone, they'd take us away from Mommy. That she's a bad Mommy and they'll find out and *take us away!*"

Her voice rose and I clutched her tighter. "No, baby. Nobody will take you away from your mom. I promise. Me and her, we're going to make sure you and your sisters are safe. Whatever needs to happen. Sometimes we have to do tough things, baby girl. You did something really hard by coming to me with this, but it was the right thing to do. I'm proud of you."

She nodded sleepily and I continued rocking her, my thoughts racing.

Randy had been doing drugs—heavy drugs—here at the trailer with his friends.

Counting tonight, they'd left those drugs where the kids could find them at least twice, and one time the twins had nearly eaten them. Then he'd taught his daughter to lie about it, and God only knew what other time bombs were still waiting to be found. Or whether he'd bring anything else over, for that matter. He still considered it his right to come into the trailer—we'd learned that the other day, when he'd broken the locks to get inside.

For all I knew, there were more baggies of this crap somewhere.

Then I heard a low, distinctive noise. Motorcycle. *Ah, shit.* I'd totally forgotten about Shade. Glancing down at my phone, I saw three text messages from him, demanding to know what was wrong. Next to it sat the bag of meth. Jesus. Randy had invited his druggie friends into his children's home. His kids could've *died*, but all he'd cared about was keeping the secret from Hannah. What the hell had he been thinking?

He wasn't.

He wasn't thinking at all, because Randy didn't give a shit about anyone but himself. Up to now I'd seen him as scum—a loser who'd abandoned his family—but that wasn't the case anymore.

Nope, Randy had just graduated to active-threat status, and I couldn't let that stand. Hannah and I were going to have to get the hell out of this trailer. It wasn't safe, not when Randy felt free to break in whenever he wanted and there was motherfucking *meth* in the bathroom. We needed to move, and we needed to move soon.

Guess I'd be claiming that five hundred bucks after all.

"Why don't you go to sleep in here?" I told Callie as the motorcycle grew louder.

"Okay," she whispered, crawling into the bed. Then I went into the living room and peeked out the window, expecting to see Shade. Sure enough, he was just pulling up outside. My hand clutched the phone and the baggie tight as he swung his leg off the Harley. Oh, shit. I needed to hide the drugs, and hide them fast.

He knocked on the door and then the knob was turning. *Crap crap crap!* The little lock in the knob must not have caught and the deadbolt was still broken. I shoved the baggie down my shorts as Shade pushed through the door.

"Hi!" I said as he took me in.

"What happened?" he asked. "I heard part of it. What the fuck's going on?"

"Nothing," I said quickly. "Callie just had a bad dream."

"Bullshit." He stepped in, closing the door behind him. "You were freaking out and you've been crying."

I reached to touch my cheeks, startled to realize he was right. They were wet. I shifted nervously, and the bag of crystals in my panties poked uncomfortably. That's when the full horror of the situation hit. There was a baggie of meth tucked up against my crotch.

Could meth go through plastic?

I had no fucking idea. I'd known plenty of meth heads—hard not to, growing up like I had—but I couldn't remember ever hearing anything specifically about whether it could seep out of a baggie and into your coochie. I needed to get the drugs hidden somewhere else. Immediately.

"Sit down," I said, pointing to the couch almost desperately. "I'll get you a drink."

Turning away from Shade, I walked into the little kitchen, trying not to waddle. Then I opened the fridge door, using it as cover to reach down and dig out the baggie. I stuffed it quickly into the vegetable drawer and then grabbed two beers.

I turned around to find him standing right behind me. Shit. How long had he been there? Had he seen anything?

"Here you go," I said, offering him a beer with what I had to assume wasn't the world's most convincing smile. "Let's go sit on the couch."

He didn't move for a minute, studying me thoughtfully. Shit. He must've seen something.

You don't know that, Wonder Woman said calmly. *It's like playing poker—you're bluffing. Don't crack.*

"Don't you want to sit down?" I asked, hoping I didn't sound desperate. Shade reached out, taking the beer. For an instant I thought he'd call me on it, but then he stepped back, holding out his arm, inviting me to go first. We'd just reached the living room when I heard the sound of a car pulling up.

"That's Hannah and Heath," I said quickly. "Um, she's not really going to like the fact that you're here. You should go before she gets pissed."

"Answer one question," Shade said quietly. "This thing you're lying to me about—are you in danger?"

"No," I said firmly, shaking my head. "Callie just had a bad dream."

"She said something about her dad and keeping secrets. You freaked the fuck out and dropped the phone. That doesn't sound like a bad dream to me."

The front door opened and Hannah stepped through, followed by her deputy. There was instant tension in the air as Heath took in the situation—obviously not a big fan of the Reapers.

The feeling was mutual, and the two men stared each other down, two alpha dogs just poised to attack. I shared a look with Hannah, willing her to play along, even though I knew she was probably pissed to find a man here. We had a strict no-sleepovers policy. I was supposed to be babysitting the kids, not fucking around with some biker.

"Did you have a good time?" I asked brightly, hoping any residual puffiness from the crying was gone.

"Great time," Heath said, his voice a lazy drawl. He wrapped an arm around Hannah possessively. "We appreciate you watching the girls."

"They were fantastic," I said, my voice unnaturally perky. "And Shade was just heading out, weren't you?"

I turned to him, begging with my eyes. *Leave. Just leave. Don't drag Heath Andrews into this.*

"Sure," he said, standing. He walked over and pulled me into his arms for a long, slow kiss that probably looked sexy as hell. I felt the coiled tension in his arms, though, and when his tongue plunged deep into my mouth it was more threat than caress. Hannah coughed behind us and I could practically feel the anger coming off her in waves.

Shade ended the kiss, dropping his mouth to my ear.

"I'm not dropping this," he whispered. "You need to tell me what happened here."

"There's nothing to tell," I whispered back. "Just go. Leave me alone."

He pulled away, raising a finger and running it along the side of my cheek, down my neck and into my cleavage. The gesture might've been flirtatious, but his eyes were cold as ice.

Then Shade turned and sauntered toward the door. When he

reached Heath, the deputy didn't step out of his way immediately. They shared another unreadable look before Heath moved closer to Hannah, wrapping an arm around her neck in a clear message of possession. Shade nodded toward the deputy then went outside, closing the door quietly behind him.

The room fell silent. My stomach churned. I took a deep breath, praying I wouldn't puke or something.

"Did the girls do okay?" Hannah asked awkwardly. Heath studied me without speaking, his face thoughtful. Suspicious? I couldn't tell.

You're probably being paranoid, Wonder Woman whispered. *Play it through. You can do this.*

"Yeah, they were great," I said. "So tell me all about it. Where did you guys go?"

"I want to check on the kids first," Hannah said pointedly, narrowing her eyes at me. "Come with me."

Way to be subtle, butthead. I nodded, smiling at Heath like a dumb bunny before following her into the girls' room. Hannah's body stilled as she realized Callie wasn't in her bed. Turning on me, she shut the door.

"She's in your room," I whispered quickly.

Hannah's mouth tightened.

"No, wait—before you get all pissy, you need to listen to me and listen carefully. Not only that, you need to not freak out or show anything on your face when you go back out there and see Heath. You're going to laugh or smile or whatever it takes to keep him happy because this is very, very important."

"What happened?" she whispered, and I could taste her sudden fear.

"Callie found a bag of meth in the bathroom," I replied. "She said that it was Randy's, and that he'd told her it was a secret. She told me a bunch more stuff, too. Real bad stuff, Hannah. Shade and I were talking on the phone and he overheard some of it, so he came over, demanding answers. I managed to hide the drugs in the fridge—I'm about 90 percent sure he didn't see anything. He's suspicious as hell, though. I was trying to get rid of him when you got home."

My sister's mouth dropped and she swallowed.

"Oh my God…" she whispered. "I—"

"We're going to take care of it," I said, reaching out to catch her shoulders, giving her a reassuring squeeze. "You and me. We always take care of things. The first step is getting rid of Heath. Then we can deal with Randy."

"I hate him. I hate that fucking asshole so much. How could he do this to his own kids? What if she'd decided to eat it or something? That could kill her."

"But it didn't and it won't. Now go out there and do what you have to do. Once he's gone, we can figure out our next step."

Hannah took a deep breath and nodded. We walked out of the bedroom and I stopped, frozen. Heath Andrews was standing in front of the open fridge. He glanced over toward us.

"I was looking for something to drink," he said, pulling out a beer. "I hope you don't mind."

"Not at all," Hannah said quickly, her voice almost hysterical. She started toward him, trying to smile. I couldn't breathe—my chest felt tight. Had he seen what was in there?

If he had, I'd take the fall. I couldn't let Hannah get in trouble for this. Trevor had lied his ass off back in Missoula, making me out to be the mastermind behind his crimes. If they came for us, I'd lie, too. I'd say the drugs were mine and make damned sure they believed me.

Going back to jail would be a small price to pay to keep the girls out of foster care.

Heath came back into the living room, taking a drink of his beer.

"I think I'll head to bed—give you guys some privacy," I said, catching Hannah's eye and glancing toward the couch. Hopefully she'd get the hint and find some way to distract him.

Heath looked between us, his eyes speculative.

Fuck.

I really, really wanted to drop this one in Future Me's lap, but for once that wasn't going to cut it. Hannah and I were going to have to figure something out, and figure it out fast.

In the bedroom, Callie was sleeping soundly, her small thumb tucked into her mouth. She gave soft, snuffly snores. She'd worn herself out crying, poor baby. I'd do anything for her. Anything at all. We'd get her through this. I didn't care what I had to do, who I had to hurt. She and the twins were all that mattered.

After about twenty minutes, I heard the front door open and then close again, followed by the sound of a car pulling away. Slipping out of the bedroom, I went to find Hannah standing with her back to the front door, as if trying to hold out the world.

"Tell me everything," she said, her eyes haunted.

Two hours later we sat next to each other, leaning back against the couch. First I'd explained everything to her, and then we'd torn the trailer apart. In the process we'd collected another baggie of meth, some pot, three pipes, and fifty bucks in cash. Now Randy's stash sat in front of us on the battered coffee table like an accusation.

"I did this," Hannah said, rubbing her temples despairingly. "I did this to us."

"No, *Randy* did it."

"I fell in love with him, though. And then I stayed with him, even when I started to suspect about the drugs. There were rumors. I just didn't want to hear them, just like I didn't want to hear about him cheating on me."

"Well, at least you were alert enough to notice the rumors," I told her, feeling utterly exhausted and wrung out. "I was oblivious with Trevor. I mean, I knew he was drinking a lot, but I honestly didn't figure out the rest until the defense attorney told me."

"It's one thing to be stupid and screw yourself over, but to expose your kids? I'm a *mother*. I can't afford mistakes like this, Mandy. What are we going to do? That is a shitload of drugs, and meth is *poisonous*. The girls could've *died*. How will we ever know if the place is safe again?"

I reached down, catching her hand and giving it a squeeze.

"It is what it is," I said steadily. "So don't waste time beating yourself up. We have to focus on the next step."

"We need to leave town," Hannah said abruptly.

"What? I thought maybe we could rent an apartment—"

"No," she continued. "You don't know Randy. In his mind, he

owns these kids and he owns me. He won't leave us alone. He'll *never* leave us alone. I thought I could handle it, but I can't. Not if I have to worry about them finding poison in their bedroom. The girls will never be safe in Violetta."

"What about Heath?" I asked, my voice low. "Maybe he could help you."

She shook her head slowly. "Randy has rights, you know. And his family doesn't have much money, but they've lived in this town for a hundred years. His parents may like me fine, but at the end of the day I'm just white trash who slept with their son. And Heath? Sure, he's a nice guy… I'm not the kind of girl someone like him sticks with, though, and you know it. Neither of us are."

She held my gaze steadily and I swallowed, because she was right. We weren't the kind of girls who had happy endings. We were the kind of girls who worked shit jobs to support shit men, and when we got arrested, everyone talked about how they'd seen it coming.

"Okay. With the five hundred bucks Bone is holding onto for me, I have six hundred and twenty total. I won't get another check until next week, but if I tell him it's a family emergency, he might cash me out early. Sara can give us a ride to Cranston and we can catch a bus from there. We're strong, Hannah. We've survived worse."

"You can't come with us," she said. "It's a violation of your probation."

"Okay, then you and the kids go. Maybe Sara will let me crash with her. Or Bone. I'll finish probation and then join you. That might be better anyway— I can keep working and send you money."

She rolled her head toward me, sighing.

"This is really happening, isn't it?"

"Yeah, it's really happening. Unless…" I swallowed, trying to wrap my head around it. "Unless you want to *try* talking to Heath, Hannah. Maybe you're wrong. He might be willing to help. He likes you a lot."

"I like him a lot, too," she said slowly, and from the pain in her eyes I knew it was true. "I might even love him. But I don't know him well enough to be sure, and once we talk to him then it's all on the record. He's a straight and narrow kind of guy. Takes his job seriously. Even if he believes us, I don't know if the prosecutor would take our side. I could lose the girls."

I sighed, my head starting to throb.

"Not only that, you'd probably have to testify against Randy," I admitted. "Assuming they believed you. Which they totally should, but...you're right. We're not the kind of girls people listen to."

"I wouldn't mind testifying against Randy," she said quietly. "But they'd ask me about the others, too, and they threatened Callie. I suppose we could try the Reapers. Do you think Shade would help you?"

"I have no idea," I replied. "I mean, he helped with Rebel. Sort of. But he also said he didn't do it because of me—it was about the fact that Rebel tried to cheat the club. I'm not sure this falls into the same category."

"I can't think anymore," Hannah said softly. "I think we need to sleep on this. Maybe tomorrow we'll have a better idea of what to do."

"Things will look better in the morning," I agreed. "In the meantime, we should probably do something with all this shit."

I gestured to the pile of drugs and paraphernalia, wondering how the hell we'd been so clueless.

"We could flush it," she said. "There may be more we haven't found, but we can get rid of this, at least. So long as it's here, we're technically in possession."

"It's as good a plan as any," I said, sighing. "Tonight I'll sleep in with the twins. That way if they wake up, I'll be right there to keep an eye on them. I don't feel like this trailer is safe anymore."

"Neither do I," Hannah admitted. "Sucks. All of it. And of course it happens right when I've finally met someone I like. We had a good thing started."

"Look on the bright side," I told her. "Maybe he's a closet serial killer. For all we know, this is saving your life."

Hannah laughed and bumped me with her shoulder. I rolled my eyes, then pushed myself up from the floor, reaching down to give her a hand.

We'd get through this.

We had to.

Chapter Sixteen

That night I had a bizarre dream that a leprechaun came to the house and peed in our milk, turning it green. Hannah laid out sticky glue traps and caught him. Then the girls tickled him with feathers until he was screaming for mercy.

He granted us three wishes.

We wished that Randy and his druggy friends would disappear, that we'd get a new house, and that they'd put in a fountain full of green milk down at the city park, because dreams are weird.

Sadly, when I woke up I was still living in a shithole that was probably drug contaminated. On the bright side, we were out of milk and had to drink hot chocolate for breakfast.

I decided to count that as a win.

After eating, Hannah and I sat on the porch and pretended nothing was wrong while we talked things over in hushed whispers. The girls played on the swing set, oblivious. When the little old lady who lived across the street came out to water her flowers, we gave her the usual smiles and waves—just like perfectly normal people living perfectly normal lives.

Unfortunately, we weren't perfectly normal people and the leprechaun's wishes had only been a dream. No matter how we looked at the situation, there were no easy answers. I had to stay put for the next four weeks or risk violating my probation. I could apply for a move, of course, but that meant finding a new place to live and a job ahead of time—not to mention coming up with an explanation that the Department of Corrections wouldn't find suspicious. That would take time, planning and money.

Hannah and the girls would have to go without me.

We had some friends up north who'd probably take them in, at least for a while. I could stay here and take my chances. Sara wouldn't mind me crashing on her couch for a few days.

"I'll ride down to the bar," I told Hannah. "Pick up that cash and talk to Bone. Ask him about an advance on my paycheck. He might be able to help."

"Okay," she said, looking as defeated as I felt. "You know, I hate this trailer and I hate Randy, but I'm really going to miss Violetta. I liked my job."

"And Heath," I added softly. "I know it's a new thing with him, but he obviously makes you happy. What are you going to tell him?"

She shrugged, her face sad. "I'll think of something. It probably wouldn't have worked out anyway. I have three kids—what man wants to take that on?"

I squeezed her shoulder, wishing I could fix it. Then I fetched my little backpack purse, grabbed my bike and started pedaling toward the bar. Two minutes later I hit the railroad tracks wrong and nearly crashed, skidding across the gravel.

Even the roads in this place sucked.

Unlike Hannah, I couldn't wait to put Violetta behind me. I wasn't even sure where I wanted to go when I left. In some ways, I didn't care. I just wanted to be free to enjoy life for a while, without constantly looking over my shoulder.

I'd passed through town and was nearly to the Pit when I heard the sound of a motorcycle in the distance. Then it drew closer, turning around the corner toward me, and I realized there were actually two of them.

Shade and his faithful companion, Dopey the Giant.

Dopey fell back as Shade veered across the road, blocking me. For an instant I considered trying to go around him. Pointless. Instead, I cruised to a stop as he cut his engine, because a confrontation was the last thing I needed.

"Where are you going? We need to finish our talk from last night."

"I needed to run by the bar," I told him, focusing my gaze on the patches listing his name and office. All of the Reapers wore patches on their leather vests. According to Bone, they were part of the code the bikers used to communicate with each other. Some of them were simple—names and towns. Others held secret meanings I'd never been able to figure out.

"Why?" he asked, and I could tell he was digging in for a fight. Crap. I didn't have time for this.

"Some dumbass left five hundred dollars there. Figured I might as well go pick it up."

Shade didn't smile, cocking his head to look at me, his stare piercing.

"What the fuck happened last night?" he demanded.

"Nothing," I told him, wishing it was the truth. "But I'm in a hurry. Get out of my way."

He shook his head slowly. "Leave the bicycle here. You're coming with me so we can talk."

"Someone will steal it."

"Not in this town. Stop fucking around, Mandy."

"Shade, I'm not—" My phone rang, interrupting us. I glance down to see Hannah's number. We usually texted each other, and she knew I was riding.

Something must've happened.

"I have to take this," I said, putting down my kickstand as I swung off the bicycle. I swiped my finger across the phone, walking away from Shade so I could answer.

"We have to leave now," Hannah said, her voice frantic. "Like, *right* now. All of us."

"Calm down," I told her in a low voice, glancing back toward Shade. He'd gotten off his own bike and was walking toward me. I turned and started walking faster. "Tell me what happened."

"Three guys showed up right after you left," Hannah said. "I recognized one of them—he used to come around and talk to Randy sometimes. The other two were strangers. They said Randy owes them money. They… Mandy, they grabbed my arm and twisted it behind my back. Really hard. I thought it was going to break. Then the bastard told me that Randy needs to pay up or they'll hurt the girls. One of the other guys was staring at Callie and it wasn't right. Like, I think he's *into* her. Wants to… Mandy, I think he wants to *do things* to her. I'm so scared. I don't think I've ever been more scared in my life."

"Fuck," I said, the words hitting me like a blow. I swayed, stunned. "You're right. We have to get the hell away from this town. *Now.*"

"I know," she said. "Call Sara. Call her right now and see if we can get a ride or borrow her car or something. I can throw some things into a backpack and—"

Abruptly, the phone was taken out of my hand. Shade caught my arm, spinning me to face him as he raised it to his ear.

"She'll call you later," he said, then hung it up. *Fucking bastard!* I slapped at him, lunging for the phone. He grabbed me by the waist from the side, then lifted me, my back to his stomach. I kicked back, trying to get him, but nothing worked. "Settle the fuck down. No phone until you tell me what's really going on."

Fury filled me. I wanted to kill him.

No, Wonder Woman said. *You have to calm down. Manage this. Work the situation and protect the girls. They're all that matters.*

Taking a deep breath, I forced myself to settle. Shade held me, leaning forward to speak directly into my ear.

"You ready to talk to me or what?"

No, I was ready to kill him.

"Yes," I managed to say, gritting my teeth. "Let me go."

He lowered me but kept one wrist held tight. Then he twisted it around behind me, forcing me into his body. He'd caught me this way the first time we kissed, but this time his eyes weren't full of heat. They were cold. Angry. I stared up at him, chest heaving, hating him and Randy and Trevor and every other man who'd ever fucked up my life.

"Tell me what happened," he said, his voice icy. It was an order, not a request. The phone buzzed and I knew Hannah had to be frantic. Shade's face was grim—he wasn't going to give up until he got what he wanted.

"Hannah's ex is causing trouble," I said quickly. "We have to leave town. Today. I'm going to pick up my money so we can buy bus tickets. You need to let me go right now, okay? It's none of your business."

His fingers tightened on me. "And were you planning to give me a heads-up about this?"

"No," I said. "I was too busy worrying about my sister and her kids. You're just a fucking one-night stand, okay?"

"Yeah, well, we never had breakfast," he said. "That means the night isn't over and you're trying to sneak out before I wake up. That's bullshit and you know it."

"It's not about you," I hissed. "It just *isn't.* You don't get a vote in this. I have to go and I have to go *now.*"

Shade let the one hand go, keeping my other wrist captive. I jerked hard, trying to get away. Might as well have been cuffed to him. He gave me the phone.

"Call your sister," Shade said, his voice softening. "Tell her I'm bringing you back to the trailer. The two of you are going to tell me everything. *Everything.* Think it through, babe. If you really need to bug out, you're not gonna get far without a car. We'll talk it over and find a solution. You can bullshit all you want about sex and one-night stands, but I'm not done with you yet and you know it. I get what I want, and I want you. If I have to deal with some drama to make it happen, then I guess I'll deal with some drama."

"This isn't drama, Shade. This is serious shit."

He caught and held my gaze. "Serious shit is what I do, Mandy. We can handle it."

There was something in his face, something strong and dangerous that almost had me believing he meant it. God, if only… I dialed Hannah's number and she picked up almost instantly.

"What happened?" she asked. "Did they find you?"

"No," I told her. "But Shade's here. He's bringing me home and then we're going to talk."

"You didn't tell him, did you?"

"Not all of it, but enough… He says we need to talk about it. Maybe he can help."

She fell silent for a moment. "He can't help, can he?"

"Honestly? I don't know," I whispered. "We'll be there in a few minutes. Try not to freak out too much. Love you."

"Love you, too."

Hanging up, I turned to Shade. The sun was behind him, turning him into a dark, looming profile of a man. Threatening. Intimidating. Implacable. *I should've stayed away from him.* I thought I'd met fun, sexy Shade, but that'd only been a front. He'd been scary Shade all along. I'd just been in denial.

"Leave the bicycle over there," he said, nodding toward a fence. "We'll come pick it up later. Then get your ass on the back of my bike."

Shade

I listened as Mandy and Hannah told me the whole story, wishing I could feel surprised. I'd seen a lot of ugly in the world, though. Far too much ugly to doubt for a second that they were in real danger. The situation didn't set right. Wasn't a big fan of pedophiles. Also wasn't a big fan of men who'd sell out their own kids for drugs.

I'd have been willing to step in on this one even if I wasn't fuckin' Mandy, and that was the truth.

As for her and her sister, they were like two kicked puppies. Mandy looked defeated. Hannah, too. All the while, her little girls were running around, playing some sort of elaborate game with sticks and leaves in the dust. I supposed they were cute enough. You know, if you liked children. I never had. Even so, the thought of some asshole touching them… Nope.

Wasn't gonna happen.

Dopey stood at the far end of the yard, smoking and giving us privacy. I'd fill him in later.

"Did he lay hands on you?" I asked Hannah, considering the situation. She looked away, one hand coming up to rub her arm self-consciously.

"He grabbed me," she admitted. "Twisted my arm. I'm more worried about Callie. The way he looked at her… This is bad. Really bad. We need to leave town right now."

"What about your boyfriend—the deputy?"

"If I call him and they find the drugs, Mandy could go to jail," she said. "It's better to leave."

"I'd rather go to jail than let them get the girls," Mandy chimed in.

"If there are drugs in the house, you're both in possession," I said flatly. "Doesn't matter who put them there. You both get arrested, those kids will go into foster care, and that sicko might come for them."

Hannah nodded, her face determined. "So we'll leave."

"Do you *want* to leave Violetta?" I asked her, considering the situation. She shrugged.

"Doesn't matter. We can't stay."

"And you?" I asked Mandy. "What about probation? You're only four weeks out from total freedom. This could destroy that."

"Hannah and the girls are all I care about," she told me, her voice resolute. "That's what counts here. If they leave, I can go crash on Sara's couch."

I nodded, already making my plans. We could handle this, of course. Randy and his little friends were like gnats to a guy in my position. I could run them off without hardly noticing. That would be too easy, though. If one of those bastards was into kids, he'd had other victims. Men like that needed to be put down. That part was straightforward enough.

More complicated was doing it in a way that let Hannah stay in Violetta. That deputy of hers was the kind of man who married a woman, took care of her. For reasons I didn't care to examine too closely, I liked the idea of Mandy's sister being happy.

That meant we had to solve the problem of the trailer—God only knew what other kinds of shit Randy had lying around.

We'd need to interrogate him, I decided. Find out exactly what he'd left there, figure out if it could be cleaned up. If he got seriously hurt during the questioning, all the better. It'd still end the same, but I wouldn't lose a wink of sleep if he bled a bit first.

"You got a place the kids can go for the afternoon?" I asked.

Mandy narrowed her eyes suspiciously. "Why?"

"Because later today we're going to have Hannah call Randy and tell him to come over. Then we're going to talk to him and you probably don't want the kids around while we do it. Might be a little traumatic."

The sisters shared a look.

"Are you serious?" Hannah asked. "Even if you dealt with Randy, his friends will still be after us. We can't pay them off. We barely have enough money to buy bus tickets north."

"I'm the president of the Reapers Motorcycle Club," I told her, my voice gentle. "Not the local chapter of the club—the whole damned thing. We got more than a hundred brothers in four states, plus all the support clubs under us. Altogether that's maybe a thousand guys, and I'll set every single one of them to hunting those fuckers down if I need to. Then I'll make sure they never bother you again."

"But—"

"They'll never bother you again," I repeated.

Hannah's eyes widened. "What will you do?"

"What needs to be done."

Both women stared at me, understanding dawning.

"Why?" Mandy finally asked, genuinely confused. I sighed, pinching the bridge of my nose.

"Because we haven't had breakfast yet," I told her.

"What?" Hannah asked.

Mandy just looked at me like she couldn't quite believe I was real.

"It means we're not done yet," I said to Mandy, catching her gaze and holding it. "And that means you're mine, at least for now. Nobody fucks with what's mine."

"We're not in a relationship," she whispered, and I couldn't decide whether she was trying to convince me or herself.

"Call it what you want. Just don't fuck anyone else while you're fuckin' me. As long as whatever the hell this is that we don't have lasts, you're under my protection. Your sister doesn't want to leave town. She's in love with that bastard, Andrews. Suck it up, Mandy, and accept some help. These are not good guys. Let me handle them and worry about definitions later."

"Okay," she whispered. "I'll call Sara—maybe she can take the kids."

"You do that," I told her. "I need to make some phone calls, too. Dopey is gonna make sure you get over there nice and safe. Then he's gonna cruise by periodically to make sure everything stays safe. You can call him if you need to, but don't unless you have to. The less of a trail we leave the better."

"We can do that," Hannah said fervently.

"Yup," Mandy agreed.

"Great. I'll be back in a couple hours with some of the brothers. We won't be riding bikes and we won't be parking in front of your place. Give me your keys now, so we can let ourselves in quietly. You got any nosy neighbors?"

"Mrs. Collins, across the street," Mandy said. "She's half blind. You won't have to worry about her. The folks on the other side are new—I don't know them very well."

"Then we have a plan. Mandy, I'll text you when it's time to come home. Just a quick message asking if you're feeling okay. You tell me yes if you're ready to go and no if you're delayed. We'll take it from there."

"What if someone sees you?" Hannah asked.

I smiled at her.

"Don't worry about me. I'm real good at this shit. Why do you think they made me president?"

Mandy

Sara was available, thank God. We'd packed the girls into the stroller with their favorite blankies and stuffed animals, on the off chance she managed to get them to nap. Not that it seemed likely, but it was the decent thing to try. She had to suspect something was up, but she didn't ask any questions and we didn't offer any explanations. She just asked us to come and pick them up by three. That's when she had to leave for work.

Shade messaged me at 12:30, and we came back to find four bikers in the living room. The first thing I noticed was that the Reapers weren't wearing their colors. I'd never seen them without the distinctive, patch-covered vests.

It was weird.

The second thing I noticed was that our living room was way too small for four big bikers. I could hardly turn around without hitting one of them. They seemed to be using up more than their fair share of the air. I knew Dopey, but the other two were strangers, and Shade didn't introduce them. They didn't waste any time, taking a few minutes going over the plan, which was mostly just Hannah calling Randy and convincing him to come over.

They'd take it from there.

"You ready?" Shade asked her. She nodded, but she looked nervous. I caught her hand, giving it a squeeze.

"Hey, Randy," Hannah said, somehow managing to hold her voice steady even though her hands were shaking. "We should talk. I found some drugs in the bathroom. You need to pick them up in the next ten minutes or I'm throwing them away."

She held the phone away from her ear as Randy exploded, shouting "Fucking cunt!" and "I'll kick your ass, you little bitch."

Nice. Classy to the end. She waited for him to run out of insults, then spoke again.

"I don't care what you think," she said quietly. "And you can yell at me all you want, but I'm not having this shit in my house. Get your ass over here and pick it up or I'll throw it away. I don't care how much money it's worth."

Another explosion, but this time it didn't last as long. We all watched as she held the phone, waiting for her chance. Finally, she managed to get in another sentence.

"Last chance, asshole. You've got fifteen minutes. Then I flush."

"Nice," Shade said, and he seemed to mean it. Hannah gave him a strained smile, sliding her phone into her pocket.

"Now what?" I asked.

"We wait. When he gets here, you'll let him in and then we'll discuss whether he's got anything else hidden in the house. After that, we'll move on to figuring out who his friends are."

"And you're sure he won't bother her again?" I asked, swallowing. It just seemed too good to be true. Too easy.

Shade offered me a feral smile. "Yeah. I'm sure."

I believed him.

Ten minutes later, Randy pulled up in his battered little car. It was some kind of hatchback that spewed black smoke every time it started and couldn't go more than fifty on a good day.

Still better than what the mother of his children had.

The bastard looked like he hadn't slept in a week. His hair was all messed up and his clothes were wrinkled. He scowled as we peeked at him through the window, stomping up onto the porch like he owned the place. I guess in his mind, he did. I glanced toward Shade, who nodded toward the door.

Hannah reached for the knob and started to open it. Randy shoved through, nearly knocking her over in the process.

"You fucking cunt," he hissed, raising a fist. "You touch my—"

"I don't think so," Shade said quietly. He'd been standing behind the door, waiting. Dopey stepped out of the bathroom, followed by the other two Reapers. That's when I realized one of them was about the same size and build as Randy, with similar coloring. Coincidence? I swallowed, making a conscious decision not to think about it.

Randy had frozen, staring at Shade with an almost comical expression of shock.

"Who the fuck are you?" he asked.

Shade smiled. "I'm the man who's gonna kill you if you don't tell us everything. Girls, go wait outside and don't come back inside no matter what you hear. And make sure nobody bothers us, okay? If anyone asks you why Randy's car is here, just say he came to pick up some of his stuff and you wanted to give him space."

Maybe it made me weak, but I was thankful for the reprieve. Randy didn't deserve our pity. Now that this was really happening, though… Well, I didn't feel good about it. But I sure as hell didn't feel bad enough to stop them, either.

Hannah and the girls will never be safe with him around, I reminded myself. *And his friends are a danger to other children, too. You shouldn't have to go to jail to protect this asshole, and your sister shouldn't have to live in fear, either.*

"Let's just sit on the porch and hang out," Hannah said. "It'll be okay. It's all going to be okay."

God, I hoped she was right.

Shade

Turned out, Randy boy wasn't quite as much of a badass when his victims weren't women. We made him strip and then duct taped him to a chair, immobilizing his hands and feet as we "discussed" the situation. It'd only taken three hits before he started crying, and then I'd pulled out my gun and pointed it directly at his head. Probably could've started with the gun, but I enjoyed punching the bastard.

He started talking so fast I could hardly follow the words, admitting that he'd hidden more meth and some other stuff in the electric baseboard heater in the children's room. Lucky thing we hadn't had a cold snap. I sent Dopey after it and smacked Randy again, this time for being such an irresponsible cockwad.

Five minutes later, Dopey came back with one baggie full of crystals and a second one full of pills. He also held a wad of cash—not much, maybe a hundred bucks—that Randy hadn't bothered to mention. Fucking moron. I had a damned gun to his head, yet he was still spewing bullshit.

"Found this in the light fixture," Dopey said, holding up the cash. I turned to Randy, seriously considering just shooting him on the spot. Unfortunately, we needed him to find the others. This guy was just part of the problem.

"I don't think you understand what's going on here," I told him. "If you don't tell me the truth—all of it—in the next ten seconds, I'm going to kill you."

His eyes widened.

"You can't!"

"Give me one good reason."

"Because I don't even know what all's in here," he babbled. "A couple of times the guys came over while Hannah and the kids were gone. They probably left stuff around, too. You'll never find everything unless I talk to them. You can't kill all of us."

I raised a brow because I damned well could kill every last one of the little bitches. I'd do it, too. Had to clean out the trailer first, though.

"We got a problem, boss." Dopey said. "Cop just pulled up."

"Fuck," I muttered, stepping toward the window.

Heath Andrews was outside, and he was moving fast. Halfway across the lawn already. Hannah and Mandy were hanging on his arms like rag dolls, for all the good it did them. From the look on his face, he knew something was off and he wasn't going to stop until he figured it out. Probably because he'd seen Randy's car, I realized. He had a whole goddamned county to cover, yet he still found time to cruise by Hannah's place every five minutes.

This was gonna complicate things. Complicate them a hell of a lot.

"Get this cockwad into the back bedroom," I said, kicking Randy's chair.

Dopey and Thrash grabbed it, dragging it toward the hallway. Bax—the prospect we'd brought along to take Randy's place—scooped up the drugs and money, making for the bathroom. I raised my gun, training it on the door, realizing there was no fucking way we could cover this up.

It crashed open and I stood, waiting, as Heath Andrews stepped into the room, his own gun raised and ready for action. Hannah was right behind him, followed closely by Mandy.

I met him head on and everyone froze.

Standoff.

His eyes took in everything. I could tell that Dopey and Thrash hadn't made it to the bedroom from Hannah's low moan. Apparently seeing Randy in all his half-dressed and bloody glory was a bit of a shock. Yeah, there wasn't gonna be an easy way to explain this one.

My mind raced, searching for a solution.

With any other guy, I'd try a bribe. Unfortunately, Heath Andrews was straight up. We'd reached out to him several times already, and while most of his fellow officers were more than willing to accept a little Reaper cash on the side, Andrews had made his position clear.

He followed the law. Period.

That same law said this was assault and kidnapping, with possession thrown in just for fun. If I let him arrest us, Mandy and her sister would get pulled in as accomplices, and all three of those little girls would find their asses in foster care.

Then they'd be sitting ducks for their dad's associates.

Hell, even if I shot the fucker, odds were good the noise would draw witnesses and we could find ourselves surrounded by SWAT. Not even the Reapers could get away with killing a cop in cold blood. At least, not without careful planning.

"Girls, get the hell out of here," the deputy said, his voice steady.

"You should go, Hannah," Mandy agreed quickly. "She had nothing to do with this, Heath. It's all my fault. Go to Sara's place, Hannah. Ask to borrow her car and start driving."

"That'll make a bad situation a hell of a lot worse. Come inside and shut the door," I ordered. Hannah's eyes darted between me and Heath, frozen in indecision. "You go to your friend's house and get her car, that'll just drag her into it, too. We can still control how this plays out."

"No. We have to stop," Hannah said, her voice quavering. "It's one thing to hurt Randy. He deserves it. Heath hasn't done anything."

"Tell me what's really going on here," Andrews insisted, holding his gun steady. Something was strange here, I decided. Something off about the way he was handling this. He wasn't acting like a cop. For one thing, he hadn't stopped to call for backup. He'd barged in like an angry boyfriend ready to clean house. Out of uniform, and that sure as shit wasn't a service issue gun… Suddenly, the pieces fell into place.

Andrews wasn't just dating Hannah—he was in love with her. He'd come in here ready to handle Randy in whatever way necessary.

I was about to bet my life on it.

"Hannah's fuckwad of an ex has been hiding drugs in the house," I said bluntly, laying it all out. "Not only that, he owes people money. Some of them were here earlier looking for it. Threatened Hannah. Said they'd take the girls if she didn't pay. I'm sure you can imagine what they'd do with them. We're here to make sure that doesn't happen."

The deputy's jaw clenched and his eyes went flat.

"Hannah, is that true?"

"Yes," she replied softly.

"You should've called me," he said, his voice full of tightly banked fury.

"Mandy's on probation," she whispered. "And we've only gone out together a couple of times. I was afraid you'd throw her in jail."

"Jesus Christ," Andrews said, shooting her a quick glance. "Jesus fucking Christ, Hannah. We—no. We'll talk about that later. Right now, we focus on making this go away. How solid is your plan?" he asked me.

My hunch had been right.

"It's solid," I told him. "Everything is in place. We only brought in Mandy and Hannah to get him here and set up what happens next."

"The girls will need an alibi," Andrews said. Hannah seemed confused by what was happening, but Mandy's eyes widened in understanding and something like wonder. She'd figured it out. "I can provide that, but your club has to deal with the evidence. This conversation never happened. As far as I'm concerned, I saw the bastard's car here and stopped by to check on Hannah. Randy was inside picking up some stuff and I thought he was bad news, so I'm taking Hannah and Mandy with me. We'll grab the kids and do something that will take the rest of the afternoon and evening. Something public."

The deputy glanced behind me toward Hannah's ex. "Do what you have to do and don't give me any of the fucking details."

I exhaled slowly, part of me sure it was a trick. Logic said it was—Heath Andrews upheld the law and he didn't fuck around. Everyone knew that. But the look on his face… I knew that look. He'd decided to do something ugly and he didn't care.

"Why?" I asked, needing the words.

"Why do you think?" Heath said. "It's for Hannah—her and the kids. If you and I work together, I think we can pull it off. You'll need to burn down the trailer, though. Destroy the evidence. I can't see any way around it." He shot a glance at Hannah. "Sorry, sweetheart, but it's gotta go. The trace evidence will come back on us otherwise."

Andrews looked back to me, holding my eyes as he lowered his gun. He set it on the floor slowly and steadily, then took a step backward.

"I'm all in," he said, his voice steady.

"We burn the trailer, the girls lose everything," Dopey said in a low voice, coming up behind me. I studied Heath, considering. I hated to give up on the place, but he was right. Burning it really would be the best solution. The trailer was contaminated as hell—not just with meth, but blood and hair and a thousand other tiny pieces of evidence. People would be suspicious when Randy disappeared, but if he disappeared because he'd accidentally torched his own trailer, leaving his kids homeless…

Hannah and Mandy would have airtight alibis if they were with a cop, and it wasn't like he didn't have plenty of enemies.

"We're losing everything anyway," Hannah said slowly. "I don't even want to live here anymore. The place is contaminated—meth is poisonous and I was already prepared to leave with the kids. I don't see how it burning would be much different. I'd like to grab a couple photos and keepsakes. Anything else can be replaced."

"We'll need to do it right," I said, thinking out loud. "Get out clean. This will draw a hell of a lot of attention. We're good but nobody's perfect—how professional is your fire inspector? He know what he's doing?"

"He's the best," Andrews said coolly. "He's also my brother. You do what you have to and I can guarantee you he'll draw the right conclusions. Nobody will second-guess him."

Damn. Hadn't seen that coming. I lowered my gun, studying him. "You're surprising the hell out of me, Andrews. I thought you were the real deal. Straight cop."

"I am a straight cop," he replied, dead serious. "Don't ever try to pay me off—I'm not interested. But this isn't about money, it's about family. My brother will back me up."

"Why?" Hannah asked, her voice almost a whisper. "You hardly know me."

"I've known you for years," he said simply. "You think I need to buy groceries every damned day? I stop by the store to see you. I watched that piece of shit cheat on you and use you, but you never lost your smile. When it finally ended, I waited. I gave you time to heal before I asked you out, but there was never any question in my mind. This is serious, Hannah. We've only been on four dates, but I've known you were for me from the first time I saw you. Six years ago. You were at the park, laughing. You had on a red sundress and you smiled at me and I thought, 'That's the girl I'm going to marry.' Then I learned you were with him, and for a while I gave up on that dream. Now it's real again, and I won't let him take you away from me. He had his chance."

Hannah melted, wrapping her arms around him. Mandy watched them thoughtfully, crossing her arms. She wasn't convinced—not so much a romantic, I decided. Neither was I...but here I was, committing a series of felonies for a woman I hardly knew.

Fuckin' moron.

Then Randy the cockwad moaned through his gag, reminding me we still had serious business to handle.

"Very nice," I said, because we needed to get this shit moving. "You kids are adorable in love and all that shit, but you need to get out of here if this is going to work. You sure your brother has our asses covered on the fire?"

Heath looked up from Hannah. "Yeah. Make it look good, though. Just because we have my brother doesn't mean we want to use him. Not if we don't have to."

"Got it," I told him. "Girls, grab whatever shit you can fit in your purses and then get out of here."

Chapter Seventeen

Mandy

Heath took us to Cranston to see the latest Pixar film. It was good. Really good. So good that I cried, although some of that might've been pent-up emotion over the situation. Afterward, Heath took us all out to Applebee's. I watched him with the kids, wondering if he could actually be the real deal.

He laughed with them, teasing and playing, all the while treating Hannah like a queen.

The whole thing was so sweet I could have vomited. Hannah ate it up. Good for them. Maybe Heath wanted a big family, and Hannah sure as hell loved being a mom. No way you'd catch me bringing any spawn into the world, but whatever made her happy was fine by me.

Ignoring them, I focused on my food, plowing through a burger the size of a house. Then the little girls begged and pleaded for ice cream, and there was a long debate over exactly what sundae to order. We'd made a decision and had just gotten our order when my phone started blowing up.

Sara: I got a call from my sister. There's a fire on the flat. I don't want to freak you out but sounds like it could be your place

Hannah's phone went off a moment later, followed by Heath's. Then more messages started arriving. Heath made a tense phone call to dispatch, then looked up at us and nodded.

Show time.

"There's a fire at your trailer," he told Hannah, and Callie's eyes went wide. Hannah and I had talked about this—we hated putting the girls through trauma, but it was better than being ripped out of their beds and taken to a whole new town.

"Mommy, what's happening?" she asked. At least the twins were too busy with the ice cream to pay any attention.

"It's okay, baby," Hannah said, wrapping an arm around the little girl. "If there's a fire, we'll deal with it."

"But where will we live?"

Hannah and I stared at each other—that was a detail we hadn't had time to figure out just yet.

"Don't worry," I told Callie. "Your mama and I used to move a lot when we were your age. I know you never met your grandma, but she was real good at figuring stuff like this out. She taught us everything she knew. We'll always take care of you, honey, okay?"

"Okay," she said, shrinking into Hannah's side.

"I have a nice, big house," Heath said. "You guys can stay there tonight if there's really a fire."

Hannah's eyes flew to his.

"What about tomorrow?" Callie asked, her voice small as my phone buzzed again.

"You can stay as long as you need to," Heath told her. "All of you."

Hannah looked at him like he was her knight in shining armor. Maybe he was, although the curse of the McBride women suggested we stay cautious. He was better than Randy, that was for damned sure—and Hannah made a great damsel in distress.

As for me, at least I wasn't in jail again.

Funny, the last time my life had fallen apart, I'd gone down as an accessory for a crime I hadn't committed. Now I was guilty as hell and a cop was covering my ass.

This kind of bullshit from the justice system is why superheroes go outside the law, Wonder Woman said, her voice accusing. *You took care of your family and that was the right thing to do. Fuck everything else.*

"Let's go," Heath said. "I just got a message from my brother. I'm very sorry, but it's definitely your place that's on fire." He looked at Hannah. "We can call my mom on the way and ask her to watch the girls for a few hours, if you like."

"No!" Callie shrieked, and heads turned toward us. "I don't know her. I want to stay with Mommy."

"It's okay," Hannah reassured her quickly. "You can stay with me. It might be scary, though."

"Nothing's scarier than you disappearing," she said. "I'm a big girl."

The drive home was tense. We kept getting more phone calls, including the hardest one—Randy's parents. Hannah handled it well, telling them only the truth.

Yes, Randy had come over that day. No, she didn't know where he was now or whether he'd been there when the fire started. Yes, the girls were fine. Yes, we'd be there soon.

By the time we pulled up, the fire was mostly out, although there was still a lot of noise and fuss. The firefighters were milling around, doing cleanup, and the neighbors were all outside watching. Mrs. Collins rushed over to us carrying a blanket, wrapping it around Callie.

"I'm so sorry," she said, leaning in to me. "It all happened so fast. The flames just exploded out of the place." Her voice lowered to a whisper. "That no good man of your sister's had just left, too—I saw him come out and get into his car, then drive away. Nearly ran over my cat. He must've done something to start it. I already told the police all about it."

"That's horrible," I managed to say.

"Mandy, are you okay?" someone shouted. I spun around to find Sara running toward me.

"I thought you were working tonight?" I asked her, feeling confused and overwhelmed.

"Bone sent me," she said. "Once we started hearing things, he wanted to make sure you were okay. How are you?"

"I'm fine," I told her. "We're all fine. We were in Cranston having dinner with Heath Andrews."

"It was Randy earlier today, wasn't it?" she asked, pitching her voice low. "That's why you wanted to drop off the girls?"

"He wanted to get some stuff at the house," I said, following the script. "Hannah and I didn't want the girls seeing him because he's gotten more erratic lately. Heath saw the car outside and stopped to check on us. By then we just wanted to get away from Randy, so we left. I still can't believe this happened."

"Oh, Mandy. I'm so sorry." Sara's pretty eyes blinked at me, and I realized she was on the verge of crying. I gave her a hug, feeling horrible for lying to her. "You can stay with me if you want. Your sister, too. I know it's small, but…"

"Heath already offered his place to Hannah," I said. "But I'd feel much better staying with you, if you don't mind."

"It's fine," Sara assured me. "I've been considering getting a roommate anyway. You can borrow some clothes and stuff, too. We'll help you get back on your feet, don't worry."

I nodded, wishing my reality was even half that simple. Over the next hour, my respect for Heath grew as I watched him talking to his fellow deputies. At some point he introduced his brother and then he sat next to me while they asked questions about what'd happened. Apparently Mrs. Collins wasn't the only one who saw Randy leaving the trailer in a hurry right before it went up. They were looking for him now, but hadn't had any luck.

Finally, it was time for us to go. I bundled Hannah and the girls into Heath's car before catching a ride with Sara back to her place. She loaned me some yoga pants and a shirt, and then I was asleep on her couch.

The next day things went from chaotic to surreal. Representatives of the local Bible church—women I'd only ever met casually—got in touch to ask what sizes we wore. Later that day they brought two big boxes of clothing and toys to Heath's house, and not just castoffs. This was nice stuff—clothing that'd been taken directly out of people's closets.

Not only that, they set out change jars at both registers in the town's only grocery store. Hannah had worked there for nearly six years, and apparently she was well liked. By five o'clock, they'd already collected nearly three hundred bucks, including an anonymous Benjamin someone had slipped in without comment.

As for me, Bone messaged and said I didn't need to work that night. I went in anyway. The thought of sitting alone at Sara's house was too weird and I hadn't heard anything from Shade. I didn't feel comfortable messaging him, under the circumstances. Hanging with Heath and Sara sounded even weirder. All I wanted was to feel normal and in control. Waiting tables sounded like heaven.

Normal, boring heaven.

I could use a little normal and boring in my life.

Suz tackle-hugged me when I walked into the Pit, then started babbling about the clothing drive and donating tips. I thanked her, steadying myself as I came face to face with Bone.

"You okay?" he asked.

"I'm fine," I told him. "I mean, it sucks, but it is what it is. It's Hannah and the girls who will have a hard time—I didn't have much in the way of stuff, anyway."

Bone nodded, stoic. "I can give you some extra shifts. We'll do a fundraiser, too. This weekend."

"You don't have to do that," I told him, overwhelmed.

"This is Violetta," he said, his mouth cocking in a rare smile. "I'd do a fundraiser for anyone who lost their place, so don't take it personally."

"You're a real prince, Bone," Sara muttered.

"Get your asses punched in," he said, ignoring her. "We'll be busy tonight—the girls agreed to donate their tips to help your sister get back on her feet, and I'm matching them. Put the word out earlier, so people will come. The Reapers will be here too. You'll be in charge of them, Mandy."

I swallowed, wondering what I would say to Shade when I saw him.

The biker in question walked in just after nine. Behind him were Dopey and a bunch of others I recognized from the clubhouse, including one who'd been at the trailer. Not the guy who looked like Randy, though. Oh, wow… *They put him in Randy's clothes and had him drive the car away,* I realized. That would explain how Mrs. Collins had seen him leave.

Dopey's old lady came over and gave me a tight hug.

"So sorry to hear about your place," she said, sounding genuinely upset. If she knew what'd really happened, she sure as hell wasn't showing it. Dopey came up next to her, wrapping an arm around her.

"Let's go find a place to sit," he said. "We're all real sorry about the fire, Mandy."

Another biker slapped my shoulder, and then they were filing past me toward the back of the bar. Shade waited until they passed, catching and holding my gaze as he approached. His eyes were dark with desire and something else. I couldn't tell exactly what that something else was, and I guess it didn't matter.

He'd saved my family last night, risking his own life in the process. So far as I was concerned, he could call the shots.

"Mandy," he said, sliding his hands around my waist.

"Shade."

"Fuckin' shame about your place. When we heard that the girls would be donating their tips tonight, we figured we'd ride over. Make sure you were okay."

"I'm fine," I said, flushing. "I'm staying with Sara."

"And Hannah?"

"She's with Heath."

Shade nodded, then leaned forward into me, his lips brushing my ear.

"You'll be comin' with me after work tonight."

It wasn't a question.

"All right."

"We'll talk more when it's time for your break."

I nodded, any resistance I'd felt toward him long gone. Shade let me go, joining his brothers at the back of the bar. I grabbed my tray and followed him, ready to take their orders.

Bone sent me on break at eleven that night. Shade had spent the last two hours watching me with that same intense stare he'd given me at that first barbecue with Rebel. When I started pulling off my apron, he stalked toward me, catching my hand and pulling me down the hallway past the office. Then we were out on the back porch and he was pushing me up against the wall, thrusting one leg between mine.

My fingers tangled in his hair as his hands caught my butt, pulling me up and into his pelvis. His mouth covered mine and his tongue thrust deep. Desire exploded through me. My nipples tightened and my legs clenched around his thigh. He shifted, hips moving against mine restlessly as his mouth dropped, sucking on my neck. I moaned and rubbed myself against his leg, desperate for sensation.

Shade dropped me abruptly, then caught my arm and dragged me over to the picnic table.

"Open your jeans," he said, his voice heavy.

I glanced around, hoping nobody was watching from the darkness. But even if they were, would it matter? We'd already done this once. Following his order, I reached down and unbuttoned my fly.

"Now touch yourself."

Swallowing, I slid my hand inside to find my clit, rubbing it. Sensation flooded me as Shade's eyes held mine. I bit my lip.

"Are you wet?"

"Yes," I whispered.

"What do you want?"

"This," I said, reaching out to cover the front of his fly with my other hand. "I want this. Inside me."

"Right here on the porch?"

I nodded, rubbing my clit harder. I couldn't wait to feel him deep inside. Filling me. Stretching me and making me his.

"Give me a taste."

Pulling my hand out, I lifted my hand. Shade caught my wrist and raised it between us. Then he slowly sucked each finger into his mouth, holding my gaze the entire time. I squeezed his dick through the fabric of his jeans, then started rubbing it up and down with the heel of my hand, pressing hard. His tongue flicked against my fingertips, then he sucked them again.

Desire and tension and the need to fuck hung in the air between us—he'd committed violence to protect me and now I was his.

Something in Shade snapped, and he caught my shoulders, spinning me around and pushing me down across the table on my stomach. Seconds later, he'd jerked down my jeans and I heard the sound of his zipper opening followed by the crackle of a condom wrapper.

Laying his hand flat on the small of my back, he pinned me as the head of his cock touched my center. Then he thrust hard, filling me in one stroke, and I gasped. Shade stilled, breathing deep. I felt him throbbing inside me.

"Fuckin' love this pussy. Squeeze."

I did, clenching tight. His hips bucked into mine before pulling back. Then he slammed home again, and this time he didn't stop to savor the moment. His hands caught my shoulders, holding me down and steadying me for his thrusts. Faster and faster he moved, the head of his cock hitting my G-spot with every stroke. Wild desire flared and I heard the sound of our bodies coming together. Raw. Dirty. Wet.

"Next time, you damned well call me if you get in trouble," Shade said, his voice like gravel. The words were punctuated with his thrusts, like he was punishing me for trying to handle Randy on my own.

Maybe he was.

I should piss him off more often, because despite the brutality of it, I'd never felt anything more amazing. I'd loved it when he'd gone down on me, but this rough and wild sex was somehow better.

Maybe it was the way it hurt a little…the way his hands held me tight, forcing me to hold steady for him, taking everything he had to give, no matter what that meant. Whatever it was, the tension spiraled through me fast and hard until I hovered right on the edge of oblivion.

Shade convulsed, groaning as his hot seed blew into me. I felt the pulse of his cock as he buried himself. That was enough to push me over the edge.

My world shattered into a spiral of stars and streaks and blessed relief.

Shade leaned down over me, catching my hair and turning my head for his kiss. He was marking me, I realized. I wasn't sure why or for how long, but until he said otherwise, I belonged to him and there was no going back.

Maybe there never had been.

He'd seen me and he'd wanted me. Ultimately, he found a way to have me. That should've pissed me off, but when I thought of Randy and Hannah and the whole horrible situation, I didn't have any room left for anger.

Shade pushed himself back up, then pulled out of me, leaving my ass on full display. Suddenly self-conscious, I grabbed my jeans, pulling them up.

"I should probably get back to work," I said.

"That's fine," Shade replied. "Just don't forget who you're going home with at the end of the night."

I nodded and turned to the door. Then I stopped.

"Shade?" I asked hesitantly, staring at my feet like a chicken.

"Yeah?"

"Will you tell me what happened last night?"

"Your sister's dumbass ex left a lit pipe in the trailer," he said. "Whole damned place burned up because of it. Fuckin' shame."

"And Randy?"

He didn't answer for long seconds. My chest tightened.

"Last I hear, he took off in that little car of his," Shade said. "Asshole made a big mistake, setting that fire. I'd think a man like that would disappear if he could. Probably won't see him around again. Him *or* his friends. You and Hannah don't need to worry."

"Okay," I whispered, wondering why I didn't feel guilty.

Because he was a drug addict who endangered his family, Wonder Woman reminded me. *And his friends were worse. They hurt Hannah and threatened Callie. There's no room for guilt here.*

"Don't forget—you're with me tonight," Shade said quietly. "No more games, Mandy."

"No more games," I agreed.

We left the bar half an hour after closing.

Riding with Shade at night felt familiar by now. We were in a pack, surrounded by his fellow Reapers and their women. I wasn't sure how many of them knew what'd gone down.

What I did know was that they'd given, and given generously.

The girls had kept a running total of their tips and sure enough, Bone had matched it. He'd also handed me the five hundred that'd been sitting there waiting all this time. There was more than enough to get a new apartment, I realized. Assuming Hannah wanted one… Heath seemed to think she should just stay at his place.

We'd figure it out later.

For now, I decided to enjoy the feel of the bike between my legs and the fact that I'd already gotten laid once. Odds were good I'd be getting laid again soon.

In four weeks, I'd be done with probation.

Life was good.

I woke up the next morning to find the bed empty, just like last time. This was a bummer because I'd been hoping for some morning nookie. On the other hand, he'd given me four orgasms total last night, so it wasn't like I was suffering.

I let myself drift back to sleep, waking when I heard voices out in the corridor. Men talking. Then the door opened and Shade stepped in.

This time he wasn't holding coffee.

"I have to go," he said. I frowned because he was in full-on biker badass mode—all leather and patches, with a knife sheathed against his leg and a distracted look on his face.

"Is everything okay?"

"Yeah," he replied, walking over to the dresser. He opened the top drawer and dug around, tucking something in his pocket before turning back to me. "I can't give you a ride home. Pepper will take you."

Then he started for the door without a second look.

"Wait," I said, sitting up.

Shade turned back, obviously distracted. "What?"

"Is this it, then?"

He frowned at me. "What do you mean?"

"I guess… Is this good-bye?" I asked, and the words sounded so pathetic that I could've kicked myself. I forced a smile, determined not to look disappointed. "Is our one-night stand over now?"

Shade's expression softened. "Have I taken you to breakfast yet?"

"No," I whispered.

"Then it's not over yet," he replied. "But I really do need to go, babe. Nothing to do with you—club business. I'm the president, which means sometimes I have to handle shit."

"Okay, then," I said, my smile genuine. "Go handle shit."

"I'll text you later. Let you know what tonight looks like."

"All right."

Shade reached for the door again, then turned back. He studied me, and I wondered what was going on in his head. I was still naked, and my hair was so crazy I probably looked like Medusa. I'd tucked the sheet across my chest so at least I wasn't totally naked. He shook his head slowly.

"What?" I asked.

He didn't reply for a minute, his face serious. "Babe, you know I'm not a keeper, right?"

"Who says I want to keep you?" I asked, raising a brow. "I'm not looking for a relationship, remember? But I'm liking this one-night stand stuff… I'd be up for more of that. Have some fun together and then some morning you can buy me breakfast. No need to overthink it."

Shade nodded slowly, then turned and left the room.

You still sure about that not wanting a relationship? Wonder Woman asked. *Because if I didn't know better, I'd say you—*

Fuck off, I snapped at her. Me and Shade would have some fun together, and then Future Me would give him a smile and a laugh when it was finally over.

Future Me was tough like that.

Totally.

Chapter Eighteen

Four weeks later

"Are you ready?" Sara shouted through the bathroom door. "Bone just called. He wants us there a couple minutes early. Said he needed to talk."

"About what?" I shouted back at her, drying off my hands. I gave myself a quick glance in the mirror, just to be sure everything was right. Tight tank with a hint of bra showing? Check. Lipstick was bright and shiny, no smudges on the teeth. Combine that with my low-cut jeans and I'd be rolling in the tips.

Not that Shade would entirely approve—he liked it when I looked good, but he wasn't so into the idea of me flirting for money.

Pretty uppity for a one-night stand, in my opinion.

Of course, that one-night stand had been going for a month straight, so there was that. At some point he'd leave town—I knew it was coming. That didn't mean I couldn't enjoy him while he was here.

Me hooking up with Shade wasn't the only thing that'd happened in the last month.

Sara and I had officially moved in together, for one. Hannah didn't need me living with her anymore. Heath's family had swarmed around her like a plague of very respectable locusts, and now his mom was helping her with the kids most days. I thought the way they'd gotten together so fast was a little freaky, but then again, it wasn't like the circumstances had been normal.

Considering that I was in a long-term one-night stand with a biker who'd made it clear he wasn't a keeper, I didn't have much room to judge.

I opened the bathroom door to find Sara already outside. Grabbing my bag, I followed her to the car, wondering what'd crawled up Bone's ass. The man was impossible to read.

"We need to stop and get gas on the way in," I said as I slid into the seat. "You told me to remind you."

"Shit," she muttered, turning on the car. "We're coasting on fumes but we're late, too. I think we can make it."

"If we don't, you can call Bone and tell him to come rescue us," I said. "It's his fault we had to rush out so fast."

Sara nodded, turning her head to watch as she backed out of her duplex's driveway. The bar was less than two miles away, so we'd probably be just fine. Worst case, we could walk. Wouldn't be the first time.

By the time we pulled up to the Pit, there were only a couple cars out front. Not busy at all. I wondered if Bone would let one of us off early. Shade had messaged me saying that he had stuff to do tonight and wouldn't be around until later, but maybe if I let him know…

Sara parked the car right in front, startling me.

"Bone will shit bricks if he sees this," I said. "He wants you in the back, remember?"

Sara gave me a sweet smile. "Bone can get his back door action from someone else."

I giggled, shaking my head. "Seriously—you aren't supposed to park here. You'll get in trouble."

"If he wanted us parking around back, he shouldn't have called us in ahead of schedule."

"Fair enough," I said. "It's your grave."

We climbed out of the car and started up the steps.

"Can you get the door?" she asked, pulling out her phone.

"Sure," I replied, pushing ahead of her.

"Surprise!" a loud chorus of people shouted, and I froze, stunned. There were Hannah and Heath and the girls. A whole bunch of the Reapers and their women… Mrs. Collins, our old neighbor and even one of the church ladies who'd stopped by with the clothing after the fire. Karen something. I couldn't remember her last name, but she was laughing and smiling at me just like everyone else.

"Congratulations on finishing probation!" Hannah shouted gleefully, hugging me so violently I nearly fell over. My little nieces joined her, squeezing me around the legs.

The wicked bitch had thrown me a surprise party. Heath came up, catching my eye behind Hannah's shoulder.

"Sorry," he mouthed at me. I flipped him off, but I smiled while I did it because he really was a disgustingly great guy. Hannah let me go and then Sara was next.

"Gotcha!" she said, laughing. "This is what you get for using up all the hot water. Next time, you better save some for me if you don't want to get set up."

"I can't believe you guys did this," I said, looking around. There were so many faces, but one was missing. Shade. Disappointment hit, but I pushed it away. Just because we were sleeping together didn't mean he had time for a surprise party.

At least some of his club brothers had shown up. I'd gotten to know them and their old ladies better over the past few weeks, and I liked them. They were decent people, for the most part. Some of them were a little rough around the edges, but considering my own crimes, it wasn't really my place to judge.

"Congrats, Mandy," Bone said, handing me a beer. "You're off tonight—no work. Just enjoy yourself, okay?"

"All right," I said, still startled. "You sure you don't mind?"

"Nope, Sara and Suz have got it covered," he told me. "Get drunk, make the most of it. Just remember that tomorrow we have to do inventory. I'll make you drag your ass in here even if you're hung over."

"You're a ray of sunshine, Bone."

"I do my best."

Two hours later, I was definitely enjoying myself. Heath's mom had taken the kids home, giving me and my sister a rare girls' night out. Now I had a nice buzz going, and when Hannah suggested putting some change in the jukebox and dancing, I was all over it.

We spent the next ten minutes studying every song, even though I knew all of them by heart. She liked country, which was just ludicrous. Fortunately, Bone loved classic rock, so there were some alternatives.

I argued with her just for fun, but eventually we managed to agree on a playlist. Well, most of a playlist. Hannah had insisted on "Wicked Game" so she and Heath could slow dance. Stupid slow dances, reminding me that ultimately I was alone. *I'll just go to the bathroom when it comes on,* I decided as the first song started to play.

It'd been a long time since Hannah and I had gone dancing, and I'd forgotten how much it kicked ass. We laughed and drank and probably made total dorks of ourselves. I didn't care. It felt good to let go, and I was having so much fun that when Wicked Game started, I wasn't even annoyed with her anymore.

I could use some fresh air, anyway.

"You're a slut," I told Hannah, bumping her shoulder with mine as Heath caught her up in his arms. Then I grabbed my beer, chugging it as I watched them, the sexy music washing through me. Standing there alone, I admitted the truth.

I missed Shade.

"Hey," said a low voice in my ear. I turned to find him behind me. He'd obviously just come in from a long ride, with his cheeks all windburned and that fierce look in his eyes that I'd come to love.

"Hey," I answered, moving toward him. Shade reached around the back of my head, pulling me in for a long, hard kiss that would've knocked up a lesser woman.

"You're pretty full of yourself," I murmured when the kiss finally ended. His hands slid down my back, one wrapping around my waist while the other cupped my ass as the music washed over us.

"I hear it's a big day," he murmured, swaying with me as Chris Isaak wailed about not wanting to fall in love. "Guess this means you're finally free."

"That's me," I said lightly. "Free as a bird."

Shade pulled away and looked down at me, a shadow crossing his face. "Let's go outside."

Catching my hand, he pulled me toward the back of the bar. Sara gave me a wink as we passed by, and I giggled, feeling silly. What'd been a good night was about to get better and I couldn't bring myself to regret that—not for a minute.

Shade pushed through the door and then we were on the back porch. He stepped over to the picnic table and sat down, leaning back against it. I gave him a sexy smile and straddled him. Then I wrapped my arms around his neck.

"I like this table," I said, pressing my breasts against his chest.

"We need to talk," Shade said slowly. "I have a present for you."

I perked up. "A present?"

He smiled. "Yeah, a present. I sold that motorcycle today."

"What motorcycle?" I asked, confused.

"The one that Rebel tried to trade you for. I sold it."

"Nice," I said. "So what's my present? Let me guess, is it in your pants?"

Shade laughed, then shook his head.

"Nope, it's right here. Lean back."

I did, watching as he reached into his vest and pulled out an envelope. Then he handed it to me. "Congratulations on finishing your probation."

Smiling, I opened it and froze. There was money in there. A lot of it. Hundred dollar bills.

"What the hell is this?" I whispered, looking back up at him.

"It's the money from the bike," he said, his voice serious. "I want you to have it."

"I'm not a whore," I told him, feeling almost sick to my stomach.

"I know," Shade replied. "But now that you're free, I wanted you to have some traveling money. Options."

"That's crazy. This isn't mine."

"Yeah, it is, and you're going to take it."

"Fuck you, Shade."

"You can use it to buy me breakfast tomorrow."

I blinked at him, feeling sick as the words sunk in. I'd known it was coming. He'd never pretended otherwise, but I'd always assumed that Future Me could handle it.

Now I wasn't so sure.

I swallowed, then licked my lips. His eyes followed the movement and I felt his cock hardening between my legs. Jesus. Here he was dumping me and the guy still wanted to get laid. And wasn't I just the dumb bunny, because even knowing he was leaving me, I'd still sleep with him tonight. I'd take as much of him as I could get. Somewhere along the line he'd turned into something more than a one-night stand.

Too bad he didn't feel the same way about me.

"So," I said. "This is it."

"Will you take the money?"

"Yeah," I whispered, feeling sick. "I mean, I shouldn't, but…"

"It's freedom," he said. "You could use some of that."

Shade was right—I really could. Unfortunately, for the first time in my life I didn't want to be free. I wanted to be stuck right here. With him.

We stared at each other.

"Have you ever been to Portland?" he asked.

"No."

"That's my next stop."

"And you're leaving tomorrow?"

"Yeah," he replied. "First thing. Something came up and I have to go."

"Right after breakfast," I whispered.

"We could eat later, instead. Somewhere down the road."

"That's not funny," I told him, my eyes suddenly full. Fucking hell. I hated crying. *Hated* it.

"I'm not joking," Shade said. "You could come with me. Just because I'm moving on doesn't mean our one-night stand has to end. I'm not ready, and neither are you."

"Maybe you don't remember, but I have a real bad track record with relationships," I said, sniffing.

"Well, I got no track record with old ladies," Shade replied, his voice serious. "But I'm willing to take the risk if you are. That's what the money is for."

"I don't understand," I said, looking down at the envelope again. There had to be a couple thousand dollars in there, maybe more.

"In case at some point you decide it's time for breakfast," he said seriously. "That's your out. If you come with me, you'll have to leave your job. I'll take care of you but I know you don't want to have to count on a man. If you decide to end things, that's your ticket back home. You won't be trapped."

"You're really serious?" I asked.

"Yeah, I'm serious. I want you to come with me."

I waited for Wonder Woman to tell me what to do, but she must've been off fighting crime. I'd have to make this decision all on my own. Studying his face, I tried to read him.

"And what would I be?" I finally asked. "I mean, if I went with you."

"Free, Mandy. You'd be free."

"And you?"

He raised a brow, then shrugged. "Do you really have to ask?"

"Yeah, I guess I do," I said. Was he serious? He *looked* serious. "What will you be?"

Shade smiled.

"I'll be yours, Mandy."

"For how long?"

He leaned forward, resting his forehead against mine.

"For as long as you want me, babe. I don't have much to offer, but what I've got is yours. So are you in, or what?"

I considered the question, wondering if a girl like me really could get a happy ending.

Maybe.

There was really only one way to find out. I took a deep breath, meeting his gaze head on.

"Okay. I'm in."

Sign up for the 1001 Dark Nights Newsletter
and be entered to win a Tiffany Key necklace.

There's a contest every month!

Go to www.1001DarkNights.com to subscribe.

As a bonus, all subscribers will receive a free
1001 Dark Nights story
The First Night
by Lexi Blake & M.J. Rose

Turn the page for a full list of the
1001 Dark Nights fabulous novellas...

Discover 1001 Dark Nights Collection Four

Go to www.1001DarkNights.com for more information.

ROCK CHICK REAWAKENING by Kristen Ashley
A Rock Chick Novella

ADORING INK by Carrie Ann Ryan
A Montgomery Ink Novella

SWEET RIVALRY by K. Bromberg

SHADE'S LADY by Joanna Wylde
A Reapers MC Novella

RAZR by Larissa Ione
A Demonica Underworld Novella

ARRANGED by Lexi Blake
A Masters and Mercenaries Novella

TANGLED by Rebecca Zanetti
A Dark Protectors Novella

HOLD ME by J. Kenner
A Stark Ever After Novella

SOMEHOW, SOME WAY by Jennifer Probst
A Billionaire Builders Novella

TOO CLOSE TO CALL by Tessa Bailey
A Romancing the Clarksons Novella

HUNTED by Elisabeth Naughton
An Eternal Guardians Novella

EYES ON YOU by Laura Kaye
A Blasphemy Novella

BLADE by Alexandra Ivy/Laura Wright
A Bayou Heat Novella

DRAGON BURN by Donna Grant
A Dark Kings Novella

TRIPPED OUT by Lorelei James
A Blacktop Cowboys® Novella

STUD FINDER by Lauren Blakely

MIDNIGHT UNLEASHED by Lara Adrian
A Midnight Breed Novella

HALLOW BE THE HAUNT by Heather Graham
A Krewe of Hunters Novella

DIRTY FILTHY FIX by Laurelin Paige
A Fixed Novella

THE BED MATE by Kendall Ryan
A Room Mate Novella

NIGHT GAMES by CD Reiss
A Games Novella

NO RESERVATIONS by Kristen Proby
A Fusion Novella

DAWN OF SURRENDER by Liliana Hart
A MacKenzie Family Novella

Discover 1001 Dark Nights Collection One

Go to www.1001DarkNights.com for more information.

FOREVER WICKED by Shayla Black
CRIMSON TWILIGHT by Heather Graham
CAPTURED IN SURRENDER by Liliana Hart
SILENT BITE: A SCANGUARDS WEDDING by Tina Folsom
DUNGEON GAMES by Lexi Blake
AZAGOTH by Larissa Ione
NEED YOU NOW by Lisa Renee Jones
SHOW ME, BABY by Cherise Sinclair
ROPED IN by Lorelei James
TEMPTED BY MIDNIGHT by Lara Adrian
THE FLAME by Christopher Rice
CARESS OF DARKNESS by Julie Kenner

Also from 1001 Dark Nights

TAME ME by J. Kenner

Discover 1001 Dark Nights Collection Two

Go to www.1001DarkNights.com for more information.

WICKED WOLF by Carrie Ann Ryan
WHEN IRISH EYES ARE HAUNTING by Heather Graham
EASY WITH YOU by Kristen Proby
MASTER OF FREEDOM by Cherise Sinclair
CARESS OF PLEASURE by Julie Kenner
ADORED by Lexi Blake
HADES by Larissa Ione
RAVAGED by Elisabeth Naughton
DREAM OF YOU by Jennifer L. Armentrout
STRIPPED DOWN by Lorelei James
RAGE/KILLIAN by Alexandra Ivy/Laura Wright
DRAGON KING by Donna Grant
PURE WICKED by Shayla Black
HARD AS STEEL by Laura Kaye
STROKE OF MIDNIGHT by Lara Adrian
ALL HALLOWS EVE by Heather Graham
KISS THE FLAME by Christopher Rice
DARING HER LOVE by Melissa Foster
TEASED by Rebecca Zanetti
THE PROMISE OF SURRENDER by Liliana Hart

Also from 1001 Dark Nights

THE SURRENDER GATE By Christopher Rice
SERVICING THE TARGET By Cherise Sinclair

Discover 1001 Dark Nights Collection Three

Go to www.1001DarkNights.com for more information.

HIDDEN INK by Carrie Ann Ryan
BLOOD ON THE BAYOU by Heather Graham
SEARCHING FOR MINE by Jennifer Probst
DANCE OF DESIRE by Christopher Rice
ROUGH RHYTHM by Tessa Bailey
DEVOTED by Lexi Blake
Z by Larissa Ione
FALLING UNDER YOU by Laurelin Paige
EASY FOR KEEPS by Kristen Proby
UNCHAINED by Elisabeth Naughton
HARD TO SERVE by Laura Kaye
DRAGON FEVER by Donna Grant
KAYDEN/SIMON by Alexandra Ivy/Laura Wright
STRUNG UP by Lorelei James
MIDNIGHT UNTAMED by Lara Adrian
TRICKED by Rebecca Zanetti
DIRTY WICKED by Shayla Black
THE ONLY ONE by Lauren Blakely
SWEET SURRENDER by Liliana Hart

About Joanna Wylde

Joanna Wylde started her writing career in journalism, working in two daily newspapers as both a reporter and editor. Her career has included many different jobs, from managing a homeless shelter to running her own freelance writing business, where she took on projects ranging from fundraising to ghostwriting for academics. During 2012 she got her first Kindle reader as a gift and discovered the indie writing revolution taking place online. Not long afterward she started cutting back her client list to work on Reaper's Property, her breakout book. It was published in January 2013, marking the beginning of a new career writing fiction.

Joanna lives in the mountains of northern Idaho with her family.

Reaper's Property

Reaper's Motorcycle Club Book 1
by Joanna Wylde
Now Available

Marie doesn't need a complication like Horse. The massive, tattooed badass biker who shows up at her brother's house one afternoon doesn't agree. He wants Marie on his bike and in his bed. Now.

But Marie just left her abusive jerk of an ex-husband and she's not looking for a new man. Especially one like Horse. She doesn't know his real name or where he lives. She's ninety percent certain he's a criminal and that the "business" he talked with her brother wasn't website design. She needs him out of her life, which would be a snap if he wasn't so damned sexy.

Horse is part of the Reapers Motorcycle Club, and when he wants something, he takes it. What is he wants is Marie, but she's not interested in becoming some biker's property.

Then her brother steals from the club. Now Marie can save him by giving Horse what he wants—at home, in public, on his bike… and if she's a very, very good girl, he'll let her brother live.

* * * *

Yakima Valley, Eastern Washington
September 17—Present Day

Marie

Crap, there were bikes outside the trailer.

Three Harleys and a big maroon truck I didn't recognize.

Good thing I'd stopped by the grocery store on the way home. It'd already been a long day and the last thing I wanted to do was to run out and buy even more food, but the guys always wanted to eat.

Jeff hadn't given me any extra beer money and I didn't want to ask him—not with his money troubles. And it wasn't like I paid rent. For a guy whose entire mission in life was to smoke pot and play video games, my brother Jeff had done a lot for me over the past three months. I owed him and I knew it.

I'd already grabbed some beer and ground beef that'd been on sale. I'd planned on burgers, buns and chips for the two of us, but I always made extra, for leftovers. Gabby had given me a watermelon she'd picked up in Hermiston that weekend. I even had a big potato salad all made up for the potluck after work tomorrow. I'd have to stay up late making another one, but I could handle that.

I smiled, thankful that something in my life was going right. Less than a minute to plan and I'd figured out a meal—might not be gourmet, but it wouldn't embarrass Jeff, either.

I pulled up next to the bikes, careful to leave them plenty of room. I'd been terrified of the Reapers the first time they'd come over. Anyone would be. They looked like criminals, all tattooed and wearing black leather vests covered in patches. They cussed and drank and could be rude and demanding, but they'd never stolen or broken anything. Jeff had warned me about them lots of times but he also considered them friends. I'd decided he was exaggerating about the danger, for the most part. I mean Horse was dangerous, but not because of any criminal activity…

Anyway, I think Jeff did some web design for them or something. Some kind of business. Why a motorcycle club needed a website I had no idea, and the one time I'd asked him about it he told me not to ask.

Then he'd scuttled off to the casino for two days.

I got out of the car and went around back to grab the groceries, almost scared to see whether Horse's bike was in the lineup. I wanted to see him so bad it hurt, but wasn't sure what I'd say if I did. It's not like he'd answered my text messages. I couldn't help myself, I had to check for him, so I grabbed my groceries and walked over to the bikes to scope them out before going inside.

I don't know much about bikes, but I knew enough to recognize his. It's big and sleek and black. Not all bright and decorated the way you sometimes see bikes on the freeway. Just big and fast, with giant, fat tailpipes off the back and more testosterone than should be legal.

The motorcycle was almost as beautiful as the man who rode it.

Almost.

My heart stopped when I saw that bike, parked right on the end. I wanted to touch it, see if the leather of the seat was as smooth as I remembered, but I wasn't stupid enough to do that. I didn't have the right. I really shouldn't even be excited to see him, but I felt a rush knowing he was already inside my trailer. Things weren't smooth between us and I honestly didn't know if he'd even acknowledge me. For a while he'd seemed almost like my boyfriend. The last time I'd seen him, he'd scared the crap out of me.

Even scary, the man made my panties wet.

Tall, built, with shoulder-length hair he kept pulled back in a ponytail, and thick black stubble on his face. Stark, tribal cuffs ringed his wrists and upper arms. And what a face... Horse was handsome, like movie star handsome. I'd bet he had women coming out his ears, and the fact that he'd spent more than one night in my bed made me all too aware that his beauty wasn't just above the belt. The thought of his below-belt assets led to a brief but intense fantasy about him, me, my bed and some chocolate syrup.

Yum.

Shit. Dessert. I needed dessert for tonight. Horse loved sweets. Were there any chocolate chips? I could do cookies, so long as there was enough butter. *Please don't let him be pissed at me*, I prayed silently, even though I was pretty sure God wasn't interested in prayers where the promise of fornication played such a prominent role. I reached the door and juggled the bags, sliding most of them onto my right arm so I could turn the handle. I walked in and looked around the living room.

Then I screamed.

My baby brother knelt in the center of the room, beaten raw and dripping blood all over the carpet. Four men wearing Reapers' cuts stood around him. Picnic, Horse and two I didn't know—a big, built hunk of a man with a mohawk, and about a thousand piercings, and another who was tall and cut, with light-blond hair in short spikes. Horse studied me with the same cool, almost blank expression he wore when we first met. Detached.

Picnic studied me, too. He was tall with short, dark hair that looked far too stylish to be on a biker and bright blue eyes that pierced right through a girl—I'd met him at least five times. He was the club president. He had a great sense of humor, carried pictures of his two daughters to flash whenever he got the slightest opportunity and had helped me shuck corn the last time he'd come to visit.

Oh, and he also stood right behind my brother with a gun pointed at the back of his head.

On behalf of 1001 Dark Nights,

Liz Berry and M.J. Rose would like to thank ~

Steve Berry
Doug Scofield
Kim Guidroz
Jillian Stein
InkSlinger PR
Dan Slater
Asha Hossain
Chris Graham
Pamela Jamison
Fedora Chen
Kasi Alexander
Jessica Johns
Dylan Stockton
Richard Blake
BookTrib After Dark
and Simon Lipskar